They'd both felt it ⬚ **again at the hospit**⬚ that Ellie was in the arms of her mentor right now, because right there and then, he wasn't a mentor.

Wasn't a boss. He was just Logan and she had loved him.

That meant something.

It was like he had always been in her life and she'd been on hiatus, waiting for him to come back into it. Seeing him in neonatal had been a surprise, but it had also been expected, in a way. She'd always known he'd come back. It had just been a matter of time before they ran into each other again. Especially with the new career path she had chosen.

They fumbled backward against a door to an on-call room, pushed it open. The room was empty, not being used, but there was a freshly made bed and he lowered her down upon it, his hands in her hair, on her body, hungry for touch, hungry for her.

It felt good to be in his arms again. He felt so right.

Dear Reader,

Pregnancy can be a very scary time for any new mother. Will they get through the first trimester? Will the scans show that the baby is okay? Will there be any pregnancy difficulties? This worry is multiplied when that mother has had a previous loss, such as a stillbirth or a miscarriage.

In this story, I wanted to focus on a mother who has experienced a huge, tragic loss and how she deals with that. I hope you'll see how strong a character Ellie is, how she not only deals with finding herseif pregnant after the loss of her son, but also how she deals with reconnecting with her first true love, the demands of a new career and everything else I chose to throw at her.

Ellie is probably one of the strongest heroines I've ever written and for that I love her very much. I hope you enjoy her story, too.

Louisa xxx

PREGNANT BY THE SINGLE DAD DOC

LOUISA HEATON

HARLEQUIN® MEDICAL ROMANCE™

Recycling programs
for this product may
not exist in your area.

ISBN-13: 978-1-335-64169-4

Pregnant by the Single Dad Doc

First North American Publication 2019

Copyright © 2019 by Louisa Heaton

Printed in U.S.A.

Books by Louisa Heaton

Harlequin Medical Romance

The Baby That Changed Her Life
His Perfect Bride?
A Father This Christmas?
One Life-Changing Night
Seven Nights with Her Ex
Christmas with the Single Dad
Reunited by Their Pregnancy Surprise
Their Double Baby Gift
Pregnant with His Royal Twins
A Child to Heal Them
Saving the Single Dad Doc
Their Unexpected Babies
The Prince's Cinderella Doc

Visit the Author Profile page at Harlequin.com.

This is for all the lovely editors who have helped
me shape my stories—Charlotte, Nic, Grace,
Sareeta and Sara. I couldn't have done it
without you!

**Praise for
Louisa Heaton**

"*Reunited by Their Pregnancy Surprise* is a
compelling read about the irrefutable connection
between a man and a woman. The story grips you
from the moment you pick up the book, and you
will not want to put this one down."

—*Goodreads*

CHAPTER ONE

WITH HER NOSE almost pressed up against the glass, Ellie stared at the row of incubators. Inside babies, some no bigger than the palm of her hand, lay covered in wires, tubes and nappies and hats that seemed far more suited to bigger, stronger babies. Dwarfing them even more.

She tried to swallow, but her mouth and her throat were dry. Her heart was hammering in her chest, and her legs were feeling as though if she didn't sit down within the next ten seconds she was going to collapse.

Ellie pressed her hand to the glass to steady herself, trying not to look at the faces of the parents who sat by each baby. She didn't want to see the pain on their faces and be reminded of her own grief. At least these parents still had hope.

Being here was bad. But it was something she was just going to have to get through if she wanted to achieve her dream of becoming a doctor. The university had placed her here—in the NICU. The Neonatal Intensive Care Unit at Queen's Hospital. So she didn't have a choice.

It was just a few weeks.

I can do this.

This part of the hospital had been nicknamed 'The Nest', because all the premature babies looked like scrawny, pink newborn birds. Here they got rest, warmth, food and protection, in the hope that one day they'd fledge and leave The Nest to go to their new homes with their families.

This was a place of hope. These families would not do well if they sensed her fear, so she turned away from the glass and sank down into one of the chairs as she awaited her mentor, Dr Richard Wilson.

She'd spoken to him on the phone just last week. He'd sounded a kindly old chap. Patient, sympathetic, friendly. Which was nice, considering some of the other mentors she'd been paired with during her training. He'd spoken to her at great length about what he hoped she would get from her placement with him, where she was in her training, what year of study she was in, which wards she'd worked on before, what he would expect from her. All standard stuff, but he had sounded different. Like a kindly grandfather.

She'd almost considered telling him about Samuel, but her nerves had got the better of her, and she hadn't been sure she'd get through it without crying, so she'd decided to delay until she'd been here a while and could judge the best time to tell her story. Because he would be bound to ask questions about it. He'd want to know about her experience as a patient. What had driven her to make the choices she faced today.

Finding it hard to swallow, she dug in her bag for her bottle of water, rummaging past all the other items. Phone. Purse. Tissues with a soothing aloe vera balm in case she lost control of her tears and didn't want to look like Rudolph afterwards. Pens. Notebook. A 2014 copy of the *BNF* that a kindly pharmacist had given her free of charge. It listed all drugs and medicines, what they were used for and what their interactions were, and she didn't want to look stupid. Tampons, just in case, a packet of painkillers and emergency chocolate...

Ah! The water bottle.

She struggled to open the lid, almost burning her palm as it came unscrewed, and then she took a giant swallow.

That's so much better.

Putting the lid back on, she stashed it in her bag and checked her appearance once more. She wanted to make a good impression on Dr Wilson. Show him that she meant business and that she was here to learn and get the most from her placement—even if this department *did* scare the hell out of her.

She sat there trying to steel herself, knowing that if she could just get through this first day, then the next day would be easier. And the one after that. And then she'd get into the flow. Perhaps see that this place wasn't as scary as she believed it to be. She would get past this placement and look back at her time on it and laugh that she'd been so scared in the first place!

It was ridiculous, the state of her nerves! Allowing herself so get so worked up.

It's stupid. It's—

'Ellie?'

She heard incredulity in a man's voice and turned to see who'd recognised her, expecting it to be a case of mistaken identity. But it wasn't. Not at all.

Shocked, she got to her feet. *'Logan?'* Ellie couldn't believe her eyes. Old, painful memories whizzed by at the speed of light. Was it really him?

Her brain scrambled to try and work out how long it had been since they'd last seen each other, but her mind couldn't compute and the numbers remained unreachable. Was she overjoyed? *Yes.* Was she apprehensive? *Oh, yes.* It had been *years.* Years since she had last seen him and he'd broken her heart by telling her that he thought it best if they were just friends.

Did I ever really get over you? No.

He'd devastated her that day. Had ended all her dreams of the future back then. But perhaps that had simply served to begin making her who she was today. Stronger. More independent. Perhaps she should thank him for that first strike against her heart? It had made her ready for all the others.

Physically, he looked different. Changed from the gangly youth of their teens into a broader, more solid-looking *man.* Wider at the shoulders, with a squareness of jaw that was now more pronounced. The years had been good to him and he'd clearly thrived without her.

Would he look at her and think the same? Probably not. She wasn't the entrepreneur she'd always said she'd be. She wasn't at the top of some corporate ladder, wearing a power suit and waving a platinum card. She'd gone back to the beginning. Was a student again. She was on the bottom rung of the career ladder when she'd always aspired to be at the top.

She noticed he wore a name badge clipped to his belt—a sign that he worked in this hospital, identifying him as a member of staff. A doctor, of course. He'd left her behind to become one. His father was an oncologist, his mother had been... She struggled for the memory. Oh, yes. An obstetrician. When Logan had left her to pursue his dream of medical school she hadn't known what speciality he wanted to pursue. She hoped it wasn't this one.

'What are you doing here?' she asked, hoping he was just passing through. Maybe he was dropping off some notes for a patient and then he would be gone again. Hopefully to work in the department that was furthest from this one. Gerontology, perhaps?

'I saw the name in the diary, but I didn't think it would be *you*.'

In the diary? Why was he looking in the department's diary? Surely that was private to Dr Wilson and his staff?

A sense of dread began to filter its way into her body, but she didn't want it to show on her face. She looked up and down the corridor, past the black and white artistic photographs of babies, past the noticeboard filled with old notices that should probably have been taken down years ago. Looking—hoping—to see Dr Wilson appear.

Perhaps if she concentrated really hard she could magic him up?

But the corridor remained resolutely empty and she turned back to face Logan, her cheeks hot, smiling politely. 'I'm here for Dr Wilson.'

Logan nodded. 'You're the new medical student?'

Her smile was almost a rictus, and she couldn't stand there talking to him any longer because it hurt too much already and... *Oh, Logan!*

'Yes. I am. So, if you could just excuse me? I need to let Dr Wilson know that I'm here. I don't want him to think that I'm late.'

And if I say his name often enough it might summon him.

She pushed past him, glad to find that, yes, indeed her legs *were* still working, and were even remarkably co-ordinated.

But as she passed him their shoulders brushed, and she inhaled a pleasurable scent of soap and sandalwood, and it was like being catapulted back to when she was eighteen years old and in his bedroom, sitting cross-legged on his bed, laughing at him because he was trying on different kinds of body spray for their date night. And then she'd got up from the bed and pulled him close to inhale the scent of his skin...

'Dr Wilson isn't here.'

His voice stopped her in her tracks and she closed her eyes in despair. Heart pounding hard against her ribs, she turned back to look at him. 'No? But he's meant to be meeting me. He's my mentor.'

Logan looked uncomfortable. 'He's not. His wife...she died this weekend.'

Oh.

That was dreadful news. Terrible! What was she to do? She'd have to ring her university. Tell them she needed to be assigned another mentor.

Shocked, she began to rummage in her bag.

'What are you doing?'

'I need to phone my tutor so they can assign me to someone else.'

Where was the damned phone? It had been there just a minute ago, when she'd dug inside to find her water. It must have gone all the way to the bottom and—

'They already have.'

She looked up at him, frowning. 'Who?'

But she already knew the answer just by looking at his face. A face that looked both guilty and apprehensive. A face that she had once kissed all over in bright red lipstick whilst he slept and then taken a picture of to give him as a card on Valentine's Day. A face that she had once caressed just to see how it went from smooth to bristly around his mouth.

'It's me. I'm your new mentor.'

Her heart sank.

Ellie Jones.

It felt strange, standing there just looking at her again. As if time meant nothing—as if all those years without her had been compressed into a microsecond of time. Her hair was a little longer, but still that dark so-black-it-was-almost-blue colour. Her eyes looked wary. Tired. As if she'd seen enough bad things in the world, thank you very much. Or perhaps it was just the way she was looking at *him*?

He was very much aware that he had broken her heart once, ruined her expectations of life and let her down. So perhaps she was suspicious as to how he could be the best mentor for her? He hadn't meant to break her heart. He thought he'd done the right thing for them both and she couldn't possibly know just how much their break-up had affected him.

But he was determined, here and now, to be the best mentor she could possibly have. As far as he was concerned the past was in the past, and though he'd hurt her once he would never do so again! He was going to push her hard during this placement, so that when she left she would realise that he had tried to make up to her for his failure in the past.

It was the least he could do. If she wanted to be a doctor, then he'd make her one. The best doctor she could be.

But can I stand to see her walk away from me again?

She'd never mentioned wanting to be a doctor before. He would have remembered something like that. Hadn't she wanted to run her own business? What had changed in her life to make her pursue this path? Because it wasn't easy. Not by a long shot. But if this was what she wanted then he would give it to her.

'I'll show you where you can put your things.'

She nodded, uncertain, clearly still hesitant.

Perhaps he ought to clear the air? State his intentions?

He turned. 'Look, Ellie, I know this isn't an ideal situation for us both, but I'm going to make sure you get the best education whilst you're on this unit with me, okay? You're here to learn and I'm here to teach. That's all it's going to be. All right?'

He hoped he could remain true to his word without letting in those pesky emotions he knew were still running so close to the surface.

* * *

Rooted to the ground, she simply stared up at him. *That's all it's going to be?* What else did he think was going to happen? That she was going to fall in love with him all over again? Or that it had already happened?

He had to be crazy if he thought that. She didn't need him stating the facts of the case as if she were some simpering spinster who thought there might be a chance of romance in the air simply because they'd been in love before.

It got her hackles up.

He'd walked her to a locker, where she'd left her things, taking only a notebook and pen with her that she could slide into her trouser pocket if she needed her hands free to perform or assist with a procedure. And now she was almost running to keep up with him.

'What's the number one reason babies end up in the NICU?'

Logan was giving her a lightning tour of the unit, asking questions as he went, not giving her any time to linger or think too much. So be it. Fine. She was here to learn. She'd show him how much it meant to her.

'Prematurity.'

'And the number one condition we see?'

She hesitated and he stopped to stare at her, waiting for a suitable answer. Had his eyes always been so blue? So intense? It was hypnotic to be under his gaze once again.

'Newborn jaundice?'

He considered her answer but his gaze was still scanning her face, as if he was familiarising himself with her features. 'Tell me about jaundice. What causes it in a newborn?'

She didn't know if it was different for newborns, but when she'd been on a general surgery ward there had been a patient there who had had jaundice.

'Er…high levels of bilirubin?'

'Are you asking me or telling me?'

'Telling you.'

He nodded. 'Good. In this place, more than any other in the hospital with maybe the exception of Paediatrics, we have to be clear and firm about our diagnoses when discussing our patients with their parents. They don't want to hear *hesitation*. They don't want to hear *doubt*. They need to hear confidence and assuredness. Yes?'

She nodded.

'Okay, so what's bilirubin?'

She rifled through the files in her brain, trying to find the most efficient way of delivering an answer that sounded assured. 'A by-product of the breakdown of red blood cells.'

He began walking and again she followed fast on his heels, admiring the waistcoat that tightly encircled his middle, his flat stomach, his broad shoulders...

'And how would we notice it?'

'Yellowing of the skin—usually hands and feet. Eyes. Er...dark urine.'

'And what causes it in babies, specifically?' Now he stopped at a door that led into another room filled with incubators. Behind him she saw a row of them, one or two nurses and a few stressed-looking parents.

'The...er...liver isn't fully developed in a neonate, so it isn't as effective at removing the bilirubin from the blood.'

He nodded. 'Good. You've been reading up for this placement?'

She let out a breath. 'As much as I could along with...you know...doing assignments and things.'

'Stay on top of it. It's essential.'

'I will.'

She was a little annoyed that he was being this way—telling her what to do, being standoffish and abrupt—but she didn't want to say anything because he was now her mentor and, quite frankly, she'd had worse. But because of their personal history it niggled that *he* was the one telling *her* what to do.

'There are two babies in this next bay with jaundice, both being treated with fibre optic phototherapy. We have blankets that are laced with fibre optic cables, which shine directly onto the babies' backs. What contra-indications should we be aware of?'

She didn't know. There'd not been anything about that in the text she'd read earlier. 'Um…'

He answered for her. 'Temperature needs to be checked, and we must also make sure they don't get dehydrated.'

Of course! It was obvious now that she thought about it, and she felt like kicking herself for not knowing the answer in front of him. Her cheeks flushed red, but he didn't see because he was pushing the door open and showing her where she could wash her hands.

'Right—over here we have Bailey Newport and his mum, Sam.'

Ellie gave a nervous smile to the mum.

'Bailey is one of a set of triplets, born prematurely at thirty-two weeks. Sam had an emergency C-section, due to the threat of pre-eclampsia, but we only had one free cot, so her husband Tom is with the other two babies at St Richard's. We're hoping to get the family together as quickly as we can, but right now it's impossible to do so.'

Sam gave them a patient smile. 'It's difficult, but we take it in turns to be with each baby as much as we can. I'm expressing, but…'

Her voice trailed away as she looked down at her son and Ellie felt as if someone had punched her in the gut. Her baby was small. Thin, scrawny limbs, his body covered, it seemed, by wires and tubes. His tiny little hands scrunched up tight.

Witnessing hurt and pain like this would be the most difficult part of this placement, and she had to grit her teeth really hard and concentrate on her breathing so that she didn't let it overwhelm her.

'Bailey's taking his mum's milk well. He's one of the babies we have using the phototherapy, but his bilirubin levels are coming down nicely and we hope we can wean him off that soon.'

'That's good. Have you been able to hold him yet?' she asked Sam. She knew that was what any new mother wanted more than anything.

'Just the once. Everyone's so busy…we sometimes don't get the chance to.'

Logan looked at her directly. 'Perhaps you'd like to help Sam hold Bailey right now?'

'Really? I'd love to.'

'Okay, let's wash our hands first.'

'Ooh! Me too!' Sam beamed.

As Sam did that Logan stood on the opposite side of the incubator from Ellie and they looked at each other over the top of it. His hot gaze was full of questions and uncertainty and she wondered what he was thinking? Was he glad that she was here? As his student? Or was he troubled by it? He seemed to be looking at her as if he was really struggling with it.

She didn't think she would fall in love with him again. She wasn't after falling in love with *anyone*—not after what had happened between her and Daniel. But he could at least look at her fondly, as if he remembered the times they'd shared. As if she was his friend. He seemed to be looking at a space just off to her left now. As if he couldn't quite meet her gaze directly.

When Sam had washed her hands, she and Logan did the same and then he showed her how to open up the incubator, so that Bailey and all his tubes and wires could be safely transferred over to Mum and nothing would be caught, or twisted, or blocked.

She nodded and stood by his side, aware of his closeness, listening to his sensible instructions and trying not to think too much about how close they had been and how this was going to be the first baby she'd held since Samuel.

He'd been bigger than Bailey. Full-term, almost. Bailey seemed tiny in comparison and she didn't want to hurt him.

When the moment came she picked him up reverently, as if he was a precious Crown Jewel she was transferring to a safe, holding her breath until the transfer was done and she'd smilingly laid him in his mother's embrace.

Sam's face lit up with joy. 'Hello, little man. It's Mummy.' She glanced up with happiness, her eyes welling with tears as she looked to Ellie and Logan with gratitude. 'Thank you *so much*!'

Ellie could have stood there all day, feeling all the feelings, just watching this mother with her precious son, experiencing *that moment*. There was nothing else like it. Such a powerful image…a mother holding her child.

She'd had a similar moment herself, only hers had not been tinged with joy but with grief.

Feeling her own tears well up, she hurriedly blinked them away, wiping her eyes just in case.

Logan saw Ellie try to hide her tears and he was rocked to his core, fighting the urge to hold her. To comfort her. The Ellie he'd known had never been so emotional or sentimental. She'd been determined and strong, batting away the troubles of life with a confident smile on her face and a *you can't hurt me* shield.

It was something he'd always admired about her—especially when her father had become sick and needed that heart transplant. He'd marvelled at her stoic attitude, amazed at her strength as her father's health had continued to dwindle until the call eventually came to say that there was a heart for him.

Back then he would have crumbled under such similar circumstances, but thankfully his parents had been blessed with fine health. Something they were taking full advantage of now, in their retirement years, travelling the globe. The last he'd heard from them they'd been in Bali and had sent him a postcard of the beach there.

Perhaps it was this place? The NICU? It was a stressful environment for anyone to be in. No one wanted their family to need to come here. No one wanted to see babies covered in wires and needing machines to breathe for them, or tubes to feed them. He had to fight the feeling to reach out and wrap his arms around her and soothe her upset.

Trying to remember his own first day on the NICU, Logan thought back to his own emotions and feelings and recalled how apprehensive he'd been, how fragile the babies had seemed, how complicated it had all looked. Had he wanted to cry? No, but...

Then there'd been the day that Rachel was born. And he'd *had* to come here. Not as a doctor, but as a parent...

Perhaps instead of soothing Ellie, he ought to be toughening her up?

'Ellie, could I have a quick word outside?'

He turned to leave, squirting his hands with antiseptic gel as he did so, rubbing the alcohol cleanser into his skin and waiting for her to join him. His heart was thudding, and he knew he'd sounded stern, but he hadn't been able to help it. Her being here had thrown him into turmoil.

Ellie closed the door quietly behind her and looked at him questioningly.

'I know this is a difficult place to be,' he said, searching for the right words, not wanting to come across as harsh. 'But it's best for everyone if the medical staff—doctors, nurses and assistants—maintain some kind of emotional distance.'

'Yes, you're right.'

He almost didn't hear her whispered reply, so determined was he to make sure that she understood. 'You can't get attached in here. You can care—just not too much. Or a job like this could destroy you. Do you understand?'

She frowned. 'Is that how *you* do it? By being emotionally distant?'

Was she referring to now? Or to the past? He couldn't quite tell. One way it would seem like a genuine enquiry, the other like a slight. A comment on an inherent fault in his being. But he refused to apologise for either.

'It's the only way to survive. So why don't you take a moment to regroup and then join me in Bay Two? There's a case of gastroschisis I think you should see.'

He watched her go, wondering. Had he been too sharp? Too terse? He didn't want to be. Having her back with him like this was... *wonderful.*

It reminded him of how much he'd missed her.

Ellie stared at her reflection in the mirror, angry at herself for allowing her weakness to escape. She wanted to blame Logan, but she couldn't. She'd wanted him to treat her like any other medical student and he was. He was simply doing his job, and if she'd got emotional in any other ward her mentor would have advised her to maintain her distance there, too.

No. This was her own damned fault. Her own damned emotions. She slammed her hand against the sink in frustration, shaking her head, keeping eye contact with herself as she gave herself a really good telling-off.

Get a grip! You're stronger than this. Do you want Logan, of all people, to think of you as incapable?

Nothing had ever been able to bring her down like this. *Nothing!*

Until Samuel. And then something had changed within her. The floodgates of emotion had opened and it seemed that now every little thing could bring her to tears. Films, books... Emotional adverts—especially all those Christmas ones that told a little story. Or the ones begging for money for starving children, or children with no clean water to drink. Something about their faces... The sorrowful music... The silent tears that spoke of a pain that couldn't be heard. She felt it all like daggers in her heart, making her feel useless and hopeless. Weak and pathetic.

Her mum had told her she would change when she became a mum herself and she'd been right.

Ellie grabbed a couple of paper towels and dabbed at her face until it was dry. Then she took a couple of deep breaths to steady herself. To calm down. She couldn't afford a moment like this again.

'Right, then, Ellie. You can do this, all right?'

she said aloud, and out of nowhere came a memory of something she'd read about standing in the 'power pose'. Wide-legged stance, hands on hips, shoulders back, chin raised. Like a superhero. How it could instil belief and confidence.

So she did that for a moment, because it was easier than having to do some kind of *haka*, which would have been noisier and slightly more embarrassing.

Her reflection smiled back at her.

The power pose was working.

Accepting his place at medical school had been a double-edged sword for Logan. His unconditional offer from Edinburgh had been fantastic, but it had also been difficult. Becoming a doctor was all he'd ever wanted to do. His parents were doctors, and he'd known he'd wanted to do that all his life.

He just hadn't expected that when it happened he'd have to leave behind the woman he loved.

She'd been sitting on his bed, flicking through a magazine, completely unaware that he had momentous news to share.

'I checked UCAS today.'

She'd looked up, dropped the magazine. Sat up straight. 'And?'

'I got an unconditional offer.'

Her face had lit up and she'd screamed with delight, bouncing on his bed as if it was a trampoline before jumping off and throwing her arms around him. 'That's amazing!'

He'd held her tightly, inhaling the scent of her hair, trying to take in every detail about her. Knowing he had to tell her the next part. The difficult part.

'It's Edinburgh.'

He'd felt her freeze in his arms.

She'd pulled back to look at him, confused. *'Edinburgh?* I thought you applied to colleges here in London?'

'I did. But Edinburgh's the one to offer me a place. Remember we went up there on the train with Mum and Dad for that interview day?'

'But I thought that you said it was too far away?'

'I did, but…' And then he'd felt a small surge of anger that he was having to defend this. 'We can still see each other. It just won't be as often as we'd like.'

'No. It won't be.'

He'd looked away. Not happy to see the look of hurt on her face. He didn't enjoy seeing her sad. 'We can make it work,' he'd offered, hoping that they could.

They were so young to have fallen in love,

and they were being thrown by this, and he hadn't been sure what the best course of action would be to stop her from hurting.

After he'd left—after he'd spent his first term away—he'd felt their separation more keenly. When he'd spoken to her on the phone he'd been able to hear the pain in her voice. How much she'd missed him…how much he'd missed her.

But what could he have done about it? He'd been so busy! Inundated by assignments, lectures and placements, he'd known there was no chance of him travelling all the way back to London, and no way she could come up to him either, because he needed to work.

He'd hated listening to her cry as they said goodbye each time. He'd wanted to do something to ease her pain, to try and make it easier for her, but the distance between them had made it hard. Each phone call they'd shared had been another stab wound. He hadn't been able to wrap his arms around her. He hadn't been able to kiss her or stroke her hair the way he usually would when she was upset.

He'd begun to think about setting her free. About whether he was being cruel to continue with the relationship, knowing that she'd be waiting for him for *years*. Ellie had dreams of her own. How could she follow them if she was waiting for him? He hadn't *wanted* to lose her. He hadn't *wanted* to walk away. What if she met someone else? But he had felt it might be the kindest thing—even if it hurt them both in the short term.

He'd called her on the phone. 'We need to talk.'

A heavy silence. 'About what?'

'About us,' he'd said, quietly. 'I don't think this is working. I've thought about this long and hard, Ellie, and I think it's best if we…'

'If we what?' Her voice had sounded timid.

'If we just stay friends.' It had broken his own heart to say it. To cut the cord. To let her go. But he had done it for her. So she could have a life.

'Why?'

'It's impossible, what we're doing. You're just *waiting for me*, Ellie, and that's wrong. You're waiting for me to finish med school. And even after that I'll have to work, and being a junior doctor is long hours and overtime, day and night shifts all rolled into one. We'd hardly see each other. And then I'd be working hard to get into a specialism, so you'd have to wait for me to finish that. I can't leave you hanging on like this—it's not fair.'

Each word had been like a scar on his heart. He'd loved Ellie so much! But he'd had to do it.

He couldn't expect her to wait for him. They were going to be apart for *five years*! And they were both so young, with so much ahead of them. It had been wrong of him to think that they could do this.

Ellie had cried down the phone, begging and pleading with him to change his mind, and although it pained him to let her go, he'd known it was the right thing for her.

When the call had finally been over, he'd put his head in his hands and just felt exhausted. He'd loved Ellie—he really had. But she needed to live her life, too. Not waste it. And he'd wanted her to be happy. Short-term pain for long-term gain, and if at the end of five years he returned home and the spark was still there then maybe they could revisit what they both wanted.

That was what he'd genuinely thought.

But five years later he'd already met Jo. And she'd been a junior doctor, like him, and she'd understood the life and was going through the same thing, and they'd just clicked, and…

And now Ellie was back and he was in turmoil. His emotions were all over the place at just seeing her.

She still had that long, wavy black hair. It concealed her face now, as she concentrated on getting a butterfly needle into the crook of the baby's arm.

'Adjust the angle. A little lower. That's it.'

The needle slid into position and she attached the vacutainers to get the required blood samples.

She had steady hands. That was good. And she'd found the vein first time, which was sometimes hard to do on babies because they were so small.

He watched her finish off and cover the needle entry point with a small wad of cotton wool that she taped into position. 'Okay, get those sent off to Pathology as soon as you've filled in the patient details.'

Ellie gave him a brief smile and he watched her walk away to the desk. Why couldn't he stop staring at her? Just having her there was remarkable, but he found himself wanting to be closer. To touch her. Make sure that she was real.

He'd made the right decision in leaving her years ago—he knew he had. There'd been no other choice.

That was years ago. Nothing you can do about it now except give her the best education you can.

She looked up, caught his eye, and he gave her a brief smile. Fate had thrown them back together again, and if that wasn't some sort of sign that this was a chance for him to make amends then he didn't know what was.

He'd set her free once. Now he would do so again. But this time when she left in a few weeks she would *thank* him.

CHAPTER TWO

'THIS IS LILY MAE BURKE. Born at twenty-seven weeks, she weighed one and a half pounds.'

Ellie gazed down at the tiny baby swamped, it seemed, by wires and tubes, wearing a yellow knitted hat that was almost too big and a nappy that seemed the same. Her eyes were covered by gauze pads and a tube was taped to her mouth, with a thinner one running into her left nostril. She looked lighter than a feather, but she was sleeping peacefully. Someone had placed a pink teddy in the far corner of her incubator.

'What happened?'

'Her mother went into an early labour at twenty-one weeks. They were able to stop the contractions and she went home—only to wake one night a few weeks later to find her bedsheets soaked through and with the urge to push. We couldn't stop the labour a second time.'

'Was it cervical insufficiency?'

'We believe so.'

'How's the mother?'

'Jeanette is here most days—you'll proba-bly meet her later. We've been getting them to do some skin-to-skin therapy, which they both seem to enjoy.'

Skin-to-skin was something Ellie wished *she'd* had the opportunity to do—one thing for Samuel before he...

The thought almost made the tears come, but there was no room for that here. She needed to hold it together.

Logan moved on to the next incubator. 'This is Aanchal Sealy. A twin born at twenty-eight weeks. He's the bigger twin and suffered from Twin-to-Twin Transfusion Syndrome. Do you know what that is?'

Ellie nodded. 'A condition that can affect identical twins who share a placenta. One twin gets more blood volume than the other.'

He nodded. Pleased. 'That's right. And alongside Aanchal is her sister Devyani—the smaller twin.'

'By how much?'

'Two whole pounds.'

'That's a lot.'

'It is. Do you know the mortality rate?'

She shook her head. 'No.'

'Sixty to one hundred percent. Do you know the dangers for each twin?'

She thought for a moment. Before coming here she'd tried to read a few of her textbooks and learn about some of the more common conditions she might come across. 'Er...the bigger twin could have heart problems.'

'That's right. What kind?'

'Heart failure.' She tried to sound sure of her answers.

'Good—you've been doing your homework.'

'Did the mother have surgery before the birth to try and adjust the blood-flow?'

'Yes, she did. An umbilical cord occlusion to try and ligate the cord and interrupt the flow of blood between the two foetuses. It has an eighty-five percent survival rate, but a five percent chance of causing cerebral palsy.'

'Does Aanchal or Devyani have cerebral palsy?'

'We can't be sure just yet.'

Logan moved on to the fourth and final baby in this room.

'And this fine fellow is Matthew Wentworth, born at thirty weeks. He's had a few problems with his oxygen levels, so we're keeping him in a high-flow oxygen box.'

Matthew was much bigger than the others.

He almost looked healthy in comparison, but she knew that looks could be deceptive.

She looked about the room—at the equipment, the machines. It was all so overwhelming. So frightening.

Samuel had never made it to a room such as this. But she wished that he had. Because if he'd made it there he might have had a chance.

These babies—they all had a chance at life. Hope was still alive for each and every one of them, and she envied them—then felt guilty for doing so. The parents of these babies probably wished they'd never had to come here, and here she was wishing she'd had the chance to. Wasn't that terrible?

Logan's dark brown eyes were staring into her soul, as if trying to read her, and she had to look away. The intensity of his gaze was too much. He'd looked at her like that before, but back then she'd been able to settle into his arms, or kiss him, or squeeze him tight. Not now, though.

How did he cope with this? Seeing all these babies who could grow up with disabilities, knowing how hard their lives and the lives of their parents might be. How did he cope, knowing that? Where did he find the strength?

What if there was an emergency? What if one of the many alarms on these incubators started to sound? What then? Would she be able to stay and watch as they tried to fight for a child's life?

I can do this. I've already survived the worst that life can throw at me and I'm still standing.

'How do you do it?' she asked him. 'Deal with this every day?'

'It's my job.'

'I know…but why choose *this* as a specialism?'

He looked around them at the incubators, at the babies, his gaze softening as he stared at their tiny bodies. 'They're so helpless, these babies. How could I ever walk away from them? Choose something else? They can't talk—they can't say what they need. You have to know. You have to be certain of what you're doing and have conviction in your actions. These babies need us. Once I'd spent a rotation here I knew I wouldn't ever want to do anything else.'

He had a faraway look in his eyes and she got the feeling that he wasn't just talking about the babies here. He meant something else. Something she wasn't privy to.

Would she always be a stranger in his life now? Or would her time here create a friendship between them so that they could go back to talking to each other about anything, the way they'd used to?

She'd missed him so much after he'd left for medical school. He'd broken her heart, and as well as losing her boyfriend she'd also lost her best friend. There'd been so much she'd missed telling him in the days after he'd broken it off. And she'd hated that empty feeling she'd felt inside because she couldn't just pick up the phone and tell him what was going on in her life.

'It's lunch. You should take the opportunity to eat whilst you can. I'd like you to have enough strength for surgery this afternoon.'

'I'm going into *surgery*?'

'Just to observe. We're hoping to help the gastroschisis baby get all her organs back in her abdomen, where they should be.'

She nodded. 'That's brilliant news.'

'Be back for two o clock.'

Ellie decided to offer an olive branch—to try and make things less awkward. 'You could join me? It would be good to catch up, wouldn't it?'

She saw the indecision in his eyes. 'Maybe another time. I have someone I need to see.'

'Oh, right. Okay.'

And she watched him walk away.

Perhaps hoping for friendship was hoping for too much?

Logan sat opposite his daughter, smiling as he listened to her tell him about blood. Specifically how many pints there were in the body and what constituents made it.

'Plasma, red blood cells, white blood cells, platelets…' She listed them off, holding her fingers out in front of her as she counted and explained their jobs.

It was a topic that anyone might talk about in a hospital and not have anyone stare, but here in a small coffee shop, just down the road from the hospital, his six-year-old daughter Rachel was drawing a few looks from some older members of the community, who appeared to be a little disturbed at her topic of conversation.

He was used to it, of course. This was one of Rachel's favourite topics. The human body and how it worked—its components and what jobs they did. It was something she'd become fascinated by ever since she'd truly begun to understand that her mother had died, and her autism had sent her down a road of trying to understand *why* her mother's body had failed.

He'd found it quite morbid to begin with. Disturbing and upsetting. So he got why strangers might find it odd. But he almost found comfort in it now, the same way Rachel did, as they settled in to a familiar, reassuring conversation in which there were no surprises and Rachel could control it, knowing the outcome.

First she would talk about blood. Then she

would talk about the heart. And then she would talk about what stopped a heart and specifically what happened after the heart stopped beating.

He could see so much of her mother in her features. Rachel had Jo's eyes. Blue, like the sky on a clear, hot summer's day. And her hair was the colour of straw—not dark, like his. Sometimes when she talked, happily chatting away about her favourite subject, he would see Jo in her and would suddenly become aware of his loss—almost as if it was fresh once again—and he would have to take a moment just to breathe and remind himself that it had been years ago.

He felt guilty about Jo. He'd loved her—he was sure of that. But had it been the kind of love he'd felt for Ellie?

Ellie was from years ago and now she'd come back into his life. Jo would never come back, but Ellie had. He wondered what she would make of Rachel? Of him being a father?

She'd asked him why he did the job he did, but he'd not been able to tell her the whole truth. That in every child he tried to save he saw Rachel. That with every baby rushed to his department he recalled what it had felt like to be a lost parent, trailing in afterwards, hoping and praying that someone had the expertise to fix his child and make everything all right.

He'd have given his own life for Rachel, so he knew *exactly* what all those parents felt when they walked through into The Nest. Terrified and afraid...making bargains with God. He had an insight that the other doctors in Neonatal didn't have, and that was why he did this job. That was why he chose to be a mentor and teach medical students—because they needed more doctors who could save these tiny babies. To give these brand-new baby humans a future. To give them time to enjoy life.

He'd never expected he would see Ellie again, even though he'd moved back to London. So much had happened in their time apart he'd figured she wouldn't want him walking back into her life. They'd be moving in different circles. London was such a vast place and he'd just assumed she would have moved on.

Back then she'd talked about travelling the globe, seeing the world, and he'd hoped that by setting her free he would have helped her do that. Yet now she was training to become a doctor. What had provoked that?

Life hadn't even touched her. Except, maybe, for her eyes. Those beautiful eyes of hers, a cloudy blue, seemed to look right into his soul. Her eyes told a story and he wondered if it was a story he wanted to hear? She looked a little sad. The brightness and optimism that had flowed from her, that he had once enjoyed, was gone, and in its place was a reserve he had never seen there before.

His own life had thrown trauma at him in the years they had been apart. What had happened to *her*? What had she lived through—if anything?

Ellie had seemed hesitant. Was it *him*? Was it meeting him again after all these years? Perhaps, it was just shock and surprise.

He'd wanted to reach out when he came back, but it had already been five long years then, and life had got in the way, and as his life had progressed with Jo he'd felt sure that it was better for both of them if he kept his distance. He'd told himself that she would have moved on too, and that getting in touch would simply be reopening old wounds. It would have seemed odd to get back in touch just to cause her more heartache…to stir up old feelings that she must have moved on from.

He'd not wanted to seem as if he was rubbing her face in it. Not that he'd suspected in any shape or form that she was single and still waiting for him, anyway. Ellie was beautiful. He'd hoped that she'd found someone, too.

He sipped at his tea and smiled at his beautiful daughter as she continued to detail the areas of the heart. Atria. Ventricles. Mitral valve. Tricuspid valve. He heard the way she always paused before saying *sinus node* and wondered, as he always did, if she would become a doctor one day.

'And then…' she paused, considering, looking up at him. It was a strange, unexpected break in her routine. 'Daddy, how do you break someone's heart?'

He almost choked on his lunch. He had to cough, wipe his mouth on a napkin. He leaned forward, wondering where the question had come from? 'Why?'

'This girl at Verity's said that her dad had broken her mother's heart.' There was another pause as she frowned. 'How do you *do* that? The heart isn't made of glass, or china. It's muscle. It's meant to be strong, not weak.'

How *did* you break a heart?

I bet a lot of us could answer this one.

Ellie was putting on scrubs, preparing for surgery with Logan. She'd spent her lunch break reading up about gastroschisis as she'd tried to eat a sandwich, finding herself falling down rabbit holes of research as she often did, reading about one situation and sparking an interest in another.

The baby in question had a silo pouch currently covering her intestines, and she knew that after the surgery she would remain in NICU for several weeks. The intestines had been floating in amniotic fluid for months, so they would be swollen and not working very well. The baby would only be discharged once she was taking feeds well, putting on weight and excreting normally.

The surgery today was to insert the last remaining part of the intestines, remove the silo pouch and repair the defect that had caused the gastroschisis in the first place.

She was just putting her clothes into a locker when one of the nurses entered.

'Hi, it's Ellie, right? Clare. Very pleased to meet you.' Clare shook her hand. 'Is this your first surgery?'

'My first on this placement.'

'You've done some before? That's good. So I don't have to worry about you fainting, then?'

Ellie smiled. 'No.'

'Dr Riley is a good surgeon. He'll teach you a lot.'

'He already has.'

There must have been something in her tone, because Clare cocked her head to one side.

'Do you know each other?'

'From years ago. We knew each other when we were young.'

'Oh. Right. What was he like back then? Still handsome?'

Ellie tried not to smile, but couldn't help it. 'Oh, yes.'

'I *knew* it. I bet every girl in school was after him.'

'I only met him at college, doing A levels.'

'The wild years, huh?' Clare stripped out of her clothes and got into a set of scrubs. 'Before he settled down?'

Ellie looked at Clare. He'd 'settled down'? What did *that* mean? Was he married? Living with someone? For some strange reason the knowledge was disappointing. Almost upsetting. But what had she expected? That he was still single? She guessed she might have *assumed* he'd be with someone, but as she hadn't known for sure it hadn't hurt. But now…? Now that she was being told for definite…? Well, that was an entirely different beast.

She didn't want to appear to Clare as if she didn't know, so she went along with it. 'Yeah.'

'It's kind of sweet how he goes to eat lunch with Rachel when he can.'

Rachel. She's called Rachel.

Ellie slowly wrapped up her hair and placed it inside a surgical cap carefully, taking her time as she allowed this new nugget of knowledge to seep into her brain.

Rachel.

He meets her for lunch as often as he can.

That's kind of romantic. They must love each other very much.

And she felt jealous. A sudden wave of jealousy hit her smack in the solar plexus, making her feel almost dizzy and faint with the strength of it. Jealous that he had someone to love. Jealous that he had someone he could wrap his arms around and hold. Jealous that someone else now held the heart she herself had once thought was hers.

'Yes. It's very sweet,' she said, thinking it was anything but.

He could feel her watching him. Those wide blue eyes were watching his every move from over her surgical face mask. He felt tempted to look up and see, but after his lunch with Rachel and her questions about breaking someone's heart he felt guilty about doing so. He knew exactly how he'd broken Ellie's.

Luckily there was an operation to concentrate on: getting the last of Baby Darcy's intestines back into her body and the hole in her abdominal wall repaired. This would hopefully be her final surgery and would get rid of the horrible silo bag that she'd had attached to her since birth.

'How was Rachel?' she asked.

His hands paused. How the hell did she know about Rachel? He hadn't told her a thing. Had she spotted him at lunchtime with his daughter? Or was this just a case of the damned hospital grapevine at work? Probably the latter. However, he still felt irritated by it. That he hadn't been the one to tell her. And this was hardly the place to be bringing up something so damned personal!

'I'm not sure that's what we need to be concentrating on right now, Miss Jones.'

There and then he knew there was a change in the atmosphere in the operating room. Knew that those around him were all looking at him with questioning glances. Because normally he was happy to talk about his daughter and her progress. He was proud of Rachel.

He met her gaze. 'I'm sorry—that was rude of me. Rachel was very well, thank you.'

The tension eased somewhat and he continued with his work, even though he still felt bad. And he'd called her *Miss Jones*. Talk about creating an issue when there didn't need to be one! Now she'd probably spend the rest of the day calling him Dr Riley rather than Logan. He needed to change that. And quickly.

'Can you see what I'm doing here, Ellie?

More light, please,' he instructed the theatre technician, standing to one side.

Ellie moved forward to see better.

'What are the complications of a silo—do you know?'

'Er…infection and fascial dehiscence.'

'Good. You've been reading up.' He looked up at her and smiled. 'On your lunch break?'

He was pleased to see her eyes crease at the corners, indicating a smile back.

She nodded. 'Best time to cram.'

'Removing the silo now… What are we looking for?'

'We're checking that the bowel looks healthy.'

'Yes. I'm going to stretch the defect now, to reduce this final section of bowel.' He carefully placed his fingers inside the defect, checking all around, before pushing the last of the bowel inside. 'Ellie would you like to irrigate the bowel and abdomen?'

She nodded quickly and he could tell that she was grateful to do something towards the surgery.

He organised the skin for closure, starting opposite the umbilicus, sealing off small bleeds with the cautery and separating the fascia, explaining what he was doing and why.

'I'm creating a purse string suture. Irrigate the wound again, please.' *Good*. She was doing well. Her hands were steady and sure. No hesitation. 'Now I'll make a new umbilicus.' He created another purse string on the outer skin.

'It's so quick,' she said, glancing up at the clock. 'Barely twenty-five minutes.'

'And Baby remained stable throughout, which is the best thing,' he said, stepping away from the table and pulling off his gloves. 'How did you find that, Ellie?'

She pulled off her surgical mask as they went into the scrub room and her face was a mask of awe and wonder. 'Amazing! You made it look easy.'

He basked in her praise. 'You might be doing it yourself one day.'

Ellie nodded. 'Maybe.'

'Have you decided on a specialism yet?'

'I'm not sure. I'd like to do transplants—I know that.'

That was a good choice—though he was a little disappointed she didn't want to choose his speciality. 'General surgery? That's good.'

'You sound like you don't approve.'

'I do. Is that because of your dad?' Her father had had a heart transplant; he remembered that.

Ellie looked away. 'I guess…' She began washing her hands.

Logan stood watching her for a moment. He'd never felt so far away from her as he did at that moment. As if she was unreachable and he didn't know why. Maybe it was the way he'd spoken to her earlier? He wanted to put that right. Hated being at odds with her.

'I'm sorry about how rude I was to you at the beginning of surgery.'

She glanced at him. Gave a brief smile. 'It's okay. I was being nosy and it wasn't very professional of me.'

'Not nosy at all. It's just... I wanted to be the one to tell you about Rachel.'

'No one was gossiping about you.'

'I know. It's just...she's my daughter and I'm very protective of her.'

Ellie turned to look at him. 'Your *daughter*?'

'Yes.'

She laughed. 'I thought she was your—' She stopped speaking, blushed and grabbed some paper towels to dry her hands with. 'How old is she?'

'Six. Going on sixty.'

Ellie smiled and pulled off her cap. 'I'd love to meet her one day.'

'She has Asperger's,' he blurted out, not sure why he was explaining, but it was out now. However, Rachel having Asperger's was only one part of who she was—he shouldn't have labelled her as if that was *all* she was. 'And she's sweet and kind. And many other wonderful things besides.'

Ellie smiled. 'She sounds lovely.'

The rest of the day had passed almost in a blur. Doing half-hourly obs on the gastroschisis baby… Running around after the others… She hadn't got to see Logan at all after they'd done a consult in A&E. She'd wanted to talk to him more, after her little mistake about who Rachel was, but she'd ended up going home without seeing him again.

His *daughter*! *Not* his wife, or partner, or whatever she'd suspected her to be. But that still meant there was a mother to his child. Where was *she*? How come he didn't meet his partner for lunch?

She could be busy. Working hard.

I don't even know what she does. She could be a high-flying surgeon like Logan.

Of course she would be. Logan liked successful people. He'd been surrounded by them his entire life. Both his parents were doctors, he had an uncle who practised law, and a cousin who had created his first app aged just sixteen and was probably a multi-millionaire by now.

I'm happy for him.

She forced a smile to her face, telling herself this was true, but she was having a hard time with it. A small, selfish part of her had wanted him to be stuck in some kind of limbo, too. Her life had been ripped apart and now she was starting again—why wasn't he? She felt so far behind everyone else now. Constantly playing catch-up.

But why did she constantly give herself a hard time? Was it because everything she tried failed? Her relationship with Logan had collapsed out of nowhere. Being a mother had ended tragically. Her marriage to Daniel had collapsed too. Her business had failed.

But now she was trying to be a doctor, and there was no way she was going to fail at *that*!

Somehow, and without remembering climbing the stairs, she found herself in the doorway to Samuel's bedroom. Everything was as she'd left it. In limbo. Half done. Two of the walls still needed painting. The crib was still in its flat-pack. A lonely teddy bear sat in the windowsill, waiting to be loved.

It all just looked so...*sad*.

But what was the point in finishing?

Ellie closed the door and went back downstairs to make herself some dinner. She'd barely had time to eat today, what with the surgery, and then rounds, and then she and Logan had been called down to A&E to assess a patient who might have been going into early labour.

Thankfully, she hadn't. The maternity unit had managed to stop her contractions with tocolytics and Ellie had got to inject her with steroids to help with maturing the baby's lungs, just in case.

It had felt good today to be hands-on—first in surgery, then doing obs during rounds, and then later with that emergency patient. She finally felt as if she was moving *forward*—that she was achieving something. And Logan was actually a very good teacher.

She remembered how he'd drilled her on the way back up in the lift.

'*Why do we inject with corticosteroids?*'

'*It helps the baby's lungs mature.*'

'*What else?*'

'*Brain function.*'

'*What would happen if we didn't?*'

'*An early delivery would mean the baby might be more likely to suffer respiratory distress syndrome or other complications.*'

'*Side effects of giving steroids?*'

'*I'm not sure.*'

'*Studies have shown that there are no adverse effects on the baby, but if more than one course is given studies do show that some babies can be a little smaller, though there are no long-term consequences. How far apart do we give the injections?*'

'*Twenty-four hours.*'

Standing in that closed confined space with him had made her realise how her body still reacted to him. It was as if it remembered. As if it wanted to feel him against her once again. It had been a terrifying and delicious feeling all at once.

She liked it that he drilled her with questions—even over some of the simpler things they did. He was being thorough, making sure she understood the basics—because if you didn't understand the reasoning behind those, how could you understand the more complicated issues? And his questions took her thoughts away from how it had felt to hold him. To kiss him. To have him kiss her back...

She liked being tested. Liked getting the answers right. It felt good. And distractions were helpful.

Downstairs, as her ready meal of lasagne cooked in the microwave, she picked up her book on neonatal medicine and began reading from where she'd stopped at breakfast that morning.

She was happy that Logan had a daughter. That he had a happy, healthy child. He was lucky to have someone to hold in his arms.

She missed that. Being able to hold someone.

To squeeze them tight, love them, knowing that they loved you back just as much.

He was lucky.

Very lucky indeed.

CHAPTER THREE

'*DON'T TOUCH ME!*' Rachel screamed.

Logan backed off, hands palm upwards. How had he forgotten? She didn't like bodily contact, she didn't like to be touched, and he'd stupidly, unthinkingly, bent down to kiss the top of her head as he'd left her at Verity's.

Rachel was looking at him like a cornered animal, scared, her eyes darting all around. His gut twisted to see her so upset. And he'd been the one to cause it.

'I'm sorry. I didn't mean it. I forgot. I'm sorry.' He turned to Verity. 'I'm going to be late—are you going to be okay?'

'We'll be fine. You go. She'll calm down.'

He nodded, smiling a thank-you. Verity was an absolute godsend for him. A childminder who specialised in children with autism and special needs, and she was just down the road from the hospital, too. She ran a strict ship, full of routine, and all the kids enjoyed it during the long summer school holidays, but she also allowed him to turn up sometimes at lunch, to take Rachel out for the hour, so he could see her in the day.

It wouldn't be long until she was back at school, and then that would change, but for now he could do it. He hoped that if he got to see her later today she would have forgotten his little misdemeanour and they'd be able to go back to talking about blood, as they often did.

He gave his daughter a wave from the door, but she didn't see it, still in the process of calming down from his thoughtless contact. Briefly he wondered what it would be like to give his daughter a hug goodbye, like other parents did when they dropped their children off at school.

I guess I'll never know.

As he walked to work he thought back to when Rachel was a baby, and how it had felt to hold her then. Even then she'd cried, and he'd thought it was because she was crying for the mother she didn't have. That he wasn't doing it right. That he was a bad father who couldn't soothe his own daughter.

She'd been way behind on her developmental milestones, hadn't talked until she was two and a half, and because he was a doctor it had been incredibly frustrating for him. Until a paediatrician had suggested she might be autistic.

Then it had been as if a veil had been lifted, and he'd finally understood her.

It had been better for Rachel after that. Not for him, though.

When he got into The Nest he saw Ellie standing at Reception, laughing with a nurse, and he envied her her simple life. Carefree. No children. Starting a new chapter in her life.

He was suddenly hit by a wave of nostalgia, of longing for how it had used to be, sitting in his bedroom, laughing and chatting, holding her in his arms, loving the feel of her, the warmth of her smile, the way that she laughed. It was infectious, her laugh. He'd like to hear it again. But most of all he missed his friend, and having her this close again was agonising, because he wanted to tell her everything.

About Rachel...about this morning at Verity's.

About Jo.

He ached for the *ease* that they'd once had. 'Ellie?'

She looked up, saw him and smiled, and it felt just like before.

He was out here in the world, feeling all alone, and he knew that she had once loved him. Cared deeply. She'd listen. He knew it. He needed someone in his corner.

Up close, she looked to him as if she was

waiting for instructions. Keen. Eager to learn. Ready for whatever came next.

Such beautiful blue eyes. So trusting.

And suddenly he couldn't do it. Couldn't burden her. No matter how much he wanted to. He had to do this alone, as he always had.

'I want you on Darcy's case today. The gastroschisis baby? She's all yours. I want hourly observations. Report them back to me. Her Mum will be in later and I thought you could get her to give Darcy a bed bath. She'd like that. Get her hands-on. Parents like contact with their children.'

She looked pleased. Thrilled, in fact, to have a case of her own. 'I will. Thank you. Are you okay?'

He nodded. 'Tough morning.'

'With Rachel?'

How to answer? He didn't want to blame his daughter for what had been his own mistake. 'No, it was me. I screwed up.' He grimaced.

She smiled. 'I'm sure your wife will forgive you,' she said, and she turned to go and check on her patient.

She doesn't know about Jo.

He sank down into a seat, his head in his hands, knowing he had to tell her. But how to do so without coming across as if he was looking for sympathy? Because he wasn't. He was looking for...*understanding*. Ellie had used to have that in bucketloads. She'd been a good listener.

He recalled the time that he'd been so annoyed at not passing his driving test first time, convinced that the test invigilator had been unnecessarily strict, and she had listened patiently as he'd ranted and raved about the unfairness of it all.

And then another time she'd held his hand and listened as he told her stories about his grandmother, when she'd passed away. She'd even gone with him to the funeral and not once had she let go of him. Always there. Always ready. And when they'd stood by the graveside and he'd been bereft of words she'd stood with him, her head upon his shoulder, just waiting for him to be ready to go. She'd laid one hand upon his arm, gently stroking it, just letting him know that she was there for him.

She'd always supported him—and what had he done for her? He'd abandoned her. Left her behind. Disappeared for years and not got in touch. And now he expected her to still be the friend she'd once been? How selfish was that? He'd never put his needs before hers.

He placed his bag and his jacket in his office and looked at the single photo on his desk. One of Jo. She'd been facing away from him on the beach promenade and he'd lifted his camera just as she'd turned to look at him, one hand behind her ear, holding back her hair, which the wind was blowing everywhere. It was a perfect shot. Her smile captured in an instant. Her eyes looking directly at him, full of love and affection.

I failed you, too. Never loved you the way that I should have.

Was he destined to fail all the women in his life? Ellie. Jo. Rachel. When would he ever get it right?

Draping his stethoscope around his neck, he sucked in a deep breath and tried to pull himself together. He might screw up personally, but professionally he had lots of little babies depending upon him—and that he knew he could get right!

At least he would try.

'She shouldn't be here.'

Ellie looked up in surprise. Darcy's mother had arrived, entering the ward almost silently. She had been about to change Darcy's nappy, but if her mother was here perhaps she would like to do it instead?

Logan's words about parents needing contact with their babies rang in her ears, so she closed the incubator and stepped back. 'No one expects their baby to come to the NICU.'

'I didn't mean that. I meant by rights she shouldn't be *here*. At all.'

Ellie frowned. 'How do you mean?'

'Darcy's father is a married man. I didn't know that when I met him. I thought he was free and single, like me. Perfect. The perfect guy. I thought we were in love...that things were moving forward for us. Then I found out I was pregnant, and when I told him he told me he was already married. Happily!'

Darcy's mother looked up at Ellie with a rueful gaze.

'If Patrick hadn't cheated on his wife then Darcy wouldn't be here, and I wouldn't have to sit day by day beside her, wondering if my baby is going to be okay. Do you know, when I found out she had gastroschisis I thought I was being punished? For cheating.'

Ellie didn't know what to say. She gazed at Darcy's mother, seeing the hurt, the pain, the loss of her dream. The dream of having a perfectly healthy child with a man she'd thought loved her. Instead she was here alone, coping with the stresses that came with a child in Neonatal Intensive Care. All alone.

She wasn't sure of the best way to answer as a medical student. Perhaps if she were a doctor then she would know the professional way to respond. Perhaps there was a class instructing students on the best way to manage something like this?

But she did know how to respond as a parent. She understood the emotions of loss and fear and loneliness. So she stepped around the incubator and pulled the woman towards her in a hug. 'It's okay. It's going to be okay. I don't know what the future holds for Darcy, but right now she's doing really well. The operation worked wonderfully, there were no complications, and there's no reason at all why Darcy shouldn't grow up with any problems at all. She's sleeping and she's breathing well. She's a good weight, and right now she's got a wet nappy that we can change. Do you want to do it?'

Darcy's mother nodded, a tear slipping down her cheek. 'Yes. I would. Thank you. And I'm sorry for just blurting that out. I do that sometimes.'

'You're under stress. It's understandable to reach out.'

The woman nodded.

'I'm Ellie, by the way. It's nice to meet you.'

'Gemma. Thank you. You're very kind.'

'I just understand, that's all.' Ellie passed Gemma a paper tissue from the box that sat on the shelf beside her. She watched as Gemma dabbed at her eyes and blew her nose. 'It's difficult to see them like this, isn't it?'

'It's not how you imagine your first few days as a parent.'

'No... Do you understand all that's going on? Is there something you're not sure of? I could get Dr Riley who performed the operation to come and talk to you again.'

'Oh, I wouldn't want to bother him. I'm sure he's busy.'

'Never too busy to reassure a parent. Let's change Darcy's nappy and then I'll fetch him for you.'

'Thanks.'

Ellie fetched the items they would need and then helped Gemma change Darcy's nappy, lifting her gently to insert the new nappy underneath, and then she performed her first set of observations on her patient. Happy that she was stable, she set off to find Logan.

Hopefully he would be able to reassure Darcy's mother that she was doing okay and that there was a plan in place for any possible contingencies. Often in hospital patients were left waiting, not knowing what was going on, and their frustration was often passed on to their friends and relations. They often felt as if they were not privy to the doctor's decisions and processes, and Ellie knew it was important that Gemma felt that she was a part of that. Part of Darcy's progress. It would help to make her feel more in control, knowing what was happening to her daughter and why.

She spotted Logan on the phone and waited for him to finish his conversation so that she could ask him to talk to Gemma.

He looked up at her and met her gaze, and she felt the familiar stir of attraction in her gut. This man was part of her past—somewhere she didn't tend to visit—and it felt surprisingly strange that he was now going to be a large part of her immediate future, responsible for her success in this new endeavour. She had vowed never to let another man have control of her life again, and yet here she was.

She gave him a polite smile and waited.

It's only six weeks. Not long at all.

He put down the phone. 'You okay?'

'Yes. I have Darcy's first observations, but I was also wondering if you could come and talk to her mother? She's a little upset and I think she needs a bit of reassuring.'

He nodded. 'Okay. Why don't you come with me? It will be good for you to see how we handle situations like these.'

She didn't tell him that she already knew. That she had once been that tearful mother.

Lost and alone. She didn't want to tell him that though his words would bring a modicum of comfort to the mother, they would never be enough until Gemma's baby was out of the NICU, healthy, and in Gemma's arms at home, living a normal life.

She dutifully followed him back into the room and quietly listened as Logan did his best.

He was good—she could give him that. He sat Gemma down and carefully explained exactly where Darcy was in her treatment. Then he explained how Darcy had ended up in her situation, and that it wasn't her fault in any way, and then he took her over to the incubator and carefully, slowly, went through what each of the machines was doing, what all the tubes were for, what everything was measuring and when he expected to see some improvement. He made sure that Gemma understood that Darcy was strong and was doing as well as could be expected at that moment in time, so soon after surgery.

'Does that help?' he asked finally.

Gemma nodded. 'Yes.'

'If you ever feel you don't know what's happening, please ask any one of us and we will do what we can to reassure you. I don't ever want you to feel that you can't ask. All of us here are dedicated to making sure that Darcy goes home with you a happy, healthy little girl.'

He placed his hand upon her shoulder and gave her a reassuring smile.

Ellie followed him out of the room, using a squirt of hand sanitiser as she passed it at the door and rubbing her hands together. 'You were very good with her,' she said. 'I think she felt a little better at the end.'

'Communication is key here. In this unit there can't be any misunderstandings. The parents are often at their wits' end and we need to make sure they know what's going on with their children. Can you imagine what it would be like to be in that sort of limbo?'

She nodded. This ought to be the perfect moment to tell him about Samuel. But she felt it would be wrong. She was here to learn, not to get personal. And she thought that if she started it would be incredibly difficult for her to stop. The urge to tell him everything would be almost overwhelming.

I've been there! she wanted to say. *I know how it feels!* And she knew how easy he was to talk to. But they didn't have that kind of relationship any more.

Instead, she just presented him with Darcy's file. 'These are her latest observations. Kidneys are working well.'

He ran his gaze over them. 'What else do they tell us?'

She met his eyes. 'That everything's going as expected.'

He agreed again. But his gaze, as he looked at her, seemed to say something else.

'So, tell me what you know about the problems faced by babies born prematurely.'

Ellie thought for a moment. 'There are many problems. The earlier they are born, the more likely they are to have difficulties.'

'Such as?'

Logan was determined to keep asking her questions about work. If he asked professional questions then he wasn't telling her personal stuff she didn't need to hear.

'Problems with breathing, temperature control.'

'Good. What else?'

'Developmental delays. Intestinal issues, infection, hearing loss?'

He nodded, pleased. She knew more than some others they had in the department. In fact, she was doing really well. Working hard, looking after Darcy, as well as helping out with some of the other patients when called to do so.

'How are you managing the workload? University, placement, assignments?'

She smiled. 'It's a lot, but I'm getting there. Thankfully I don't have any distractions at home.'

He stared at her, intrigued by the small nugget of information she'd offered. 'You still live at home?'

'I moved out years ago. I've been living on my own for some time now.'

On her own.

Logan felt that the next most natural question would be, *Did you never meet anyone?* He hoped she had. Because he didn't want to think she'd been alone. Because surely it was impossible that there hadn't been a significant other in her life? Ellie was beautiful. Kind and caring. Loving.

He felt awkward, as if he somehow still owed her something for the way he had ended things. An explanation? An apology? It didn't feel right, having to be businesslike with her. This awkwardness between them was uncomfortable. Once upon a time Logan had felt so at ease whenever he was with Ellie. Now that seemed to be gone, and surprisingly it hurt.

'Still plenty of time for that, I guess.'

She smiled. 'Well, my work and my studies are what's important right now, so...'

'Yes, of course they are. No time for...'

Romance? Anything else?

'No.'

Clare appeared at their sides then. 'I was about to insert the NG tube into Baby Sealy Number One but I thought it might be a good procedure for Ellie to do. What do you think?'

He welcomed the interruption. Their conversation was sending his thoughts into a direction he wasn't sure he wanted them to go. Did he still harbour feelings for Ellie? Of course he did. He felt confused and conflicted around her. But after Jo he'd vowed never to get involved with anyone ever again.

Ellie's different, though, isn't she? I've never stopped loving her.

'That's a great idea. Check Darcy's obs again, and if everything's fine then help Clare, okay?'

Ellie nodded. 'Sounds like a plan.'

'Do you know why we're inserting a tube?' Clare had asked.

'I'm assuming to help with feeds?'

'Aanchal Sealy is only twenty-eight weeks and therefore doesn't yet have a sucking reflex. She has also demonstrated difficulty with swallowing, so a tube going directly into her stomach will help her feed and maintain her weight gain.'

'Okay.'

'Once you've gathered the equipment you

need, you must wash your hands. Have you been taught an effective way to do this properly?'

'Yes. We were taught that in our first week.'

'Good. So, with our patient straight, we have to measure the desired length of NG tube to be inserted. We measure from the bridge of the nose to the earlobe, then down to below the xiphisternum. Do you know what that is?'

The xiphisternum? Ellie assumed it was somewhere in the middle of the chest, but where was it exactly? 'No.'

'It's the lowest part of the sternum.' Sarah pointed at the baby's chest. 'Then we lubricate the tip of the tube and insert through the nostril.'

'Okay.'

'You have to hold the baby steady as she might struggle a little as you gently advance the NG tube through the nasopharynx. But this is the most uncomfortable part for the baby, so don't go too slowly.'

Ellie gripped the tube in her hand and steadied her breathing as she advanced it into the baby's nostril. Aanchal squirmed and tried to wriggle, but with Clare holding her firmly she managed to get it in first try!

'That's excellent! Well done. Now, once you get to the right length you can fix the tube to the cheek with a dressing.' She handed Ellie a pre-cut strip of tape. 'Remove the guide wire and you should be done!'

Ellie beamed with pride. Her first neonatal naso-gastric tube! This was what it was all about. Treating patients. Achieving targets. She'd looked in the induction pack that she'd received on her first day here and there was a list of clinical skills that she had to achieve before she left her placement. Cannulas, catheters, basic observations, drawing blood… She was slowly beginning to work through them and get them signed off. It was a real sign of how she was progressing in her career and it reminded her that she needed to focus on that, and not so much on Logan.

'Thanks, Clare.'

'Hey, no problem.'

'How long have you been a neonatal nurse?'

'A few years.'

'You must have seen it all?'

'There are days when you think you can't be surprised any more, but then you are. I guess that's medicine for you.'

'What's been your most difficult case?'

Sarah thought for a moment. 'Dr Riley's daughter.'

Ellie was stunned. *'Rachel?'*

Clare nodded. 'All cases are difficult, but

when it's one of your own it's…' She shook her head as if she still couldn't quite believe it. 'She had such a tragic start to her life. Emotions were incredibly high. But that's the way of the world, isn't it? Bad things can happen to anyone.'

Ellie wanted to ask more, but some parents arrived at that moment and Clare got up to greet them and walked away.

Ellie washed her hands, wondering what had happened to Rachel. What the tragic start to her life had been? If she really wanted to know she would have to ask Logan. But somehow it didn't seem quite right, and she knew she'd keep her questions and her thoughts to herself.

Clearly something bad had happened, but if he wanted her to know wouldn't he tell her?

At the end of the day, Ellie set out for home at the same time as Logan. They travelled down in the lift together and when the doors pinged open looked at each other uncertainly.

'Well, I guess I'll see you tomorrow?'

Ellie nodded. 'Yes. Definitely.'

'Good. Well, have a good night.'

'You, too.'

As he walked away she looked at him. He was drawing up his collar to keep out the light rain that was falling and she wondered what he was walking home to. Perhaps his wife was a good listener and she would help soothe his worries and his cares? They must work as a team, looking after Rachel. Was it difficult? Autism was a spectrum, and she had no idea how affected his daughter was. The mention of Asperger's indicated she was high-functioning, so maybe she was extremely intelligent even if her social cues were a little off.

I wonder who she looks like?

Did his daughter look like him? What would it feel like to see her? To look for those similarities? It had been awesome to see her own features in Samuel's face. Strange, but also powerful. It had bonded him to her in a way she hadn't expected, with such force it had almost taken her breath away. So to lose him so quickly had been...

Ellie pulled her umbrella out of her bag and popped it open. With one last look at Logan's retreating form, she headed in the other direction.

The baby was small—barely a pound in weight. Ellie stood back as Logan and his team swarmed around their new patient. She watched intently, trying to take it all in. She saw Logan place his stethoscope in his ears and listen to the baby's chest before he began issuing orders.

It was frightening to stand back, knowing that she could do nothing but watch. She wanted to help so much! But all she could do was stay out of the way, hugging the wall.

The team were busy with the new arrival for a good fifteen minutes. At first she thought it all seemed a little chaotic, but the more she watched, the more she noticed that everyone knew exactly what to do and when, and that Logan was leading his team calmly and efficiently. Everybody listened. Everyone respected each other and the jobs they had to do. And when it was over the baby was in an incubator, attached to a ventilator and in a stable condition.

Logan came over to her. 'I'm sorry I didn't get the opportunity to explain what was happening there. Stabilising a patient takes priority over teaching and time was critical.'

'That's okay. I could see that. What happens next?' She looked at the baby, which was pinky red. It looked so small, and she couldn't quite get over the fact that this baby was brandnew—minutes old—already facing a future filled with uncertainties.

'We'll do observations to start with, and then, when mum and dad get up here, we can talk them through what we need to be worrying about. The baby might need a scan.'

Logan went to the sink and began to wash

his hands, then dried them with green paper towels.

'A brain scan?'

'To make sure there have been no bleeds on the brain. This patient is critical.'

'Right...'

She didn't know what to do. This sounded serious. So far there'd been no emergencies in the NICU while she'd been there. What would she do? How would she cope if a baby died? Would she be able to hold it together? Somehow she'd have to find the strength, because her thoughts had to be for the baby's parents rather than herself.

She found herself staring at the tiny baby in its incubator, praying silently to herself that he'd make it through.

'These are the difficult moments. They can be hard to witness. If you think you can't handle it, then I'd rather you weren't around when the parents arrive.'

'I can handle it,' she said with determination. 'How do *you* do it?'

His eyes darkened. 'Practice.'

The urge to pull him close was strong. To wrap her arms around him and keep him safe in her arms. The feeling was so strong she almost swayed.

'You okay?' he asked, reaching for her arm.

His hand upon her had a startling effect. As if she was being seared by his touch. She couldn't bear it and pulled herself free. 'I'm fine.'

But her voice was shaky and uncertain and suddenly Logan was staring at her and mis-reading the situation.

'Better take five minutes. Go on. I can do this.'

'I'm okay, Logan.'

He smiled, his face full of empathy and kind-ness. 'I know. But take a break anyway.'

Twenty minutes later he found her in the staff room, cradling a mug of tea in her hands that looked as if it had gone cold. She looked trou-bled, and he felt the need to try and bolster her self-confidence.

'It's okay to get upset.' He sat opposite her, removing his stethoscope from around his neck and placing it on the table. 'In private, at any rate.'

'How do you *do* it, Logan? How do you look after these tiny babies? After what happened with your daughter?'

He blinked. 'You know about what happened to Rachel?'

'No. Someone said she came here, but not why.'

He nodded, thinking about telling her. He

wanted to. And this would be the perfect time to explain everything. Yesterday he had wanted to tell her so much, yet he hadn't wanted to burden her. Maybe now it was time?

'I met Jo when I came back from Edinburgh. We were both junior doctors, and both working in A&E to begin with, so we spent a lot of time together.'

'She's your wife?'

He almost winced at the present tense. 'Jo got pregnant with Rachel. We had a very quick, very small wedding. Both of us wanted to be married before our daughter arrived.'

He glanced at Ellie to gauge how she was reacting to this. She seemed absorbed in the story, so he continued.

'One day we were driving home after a busy shift together and another driver…he had been up all night drinking…ploughed into our vehicle, side-on. He flipped us up, over and over, and the car came to rest on its roof.

'Oh, my God…'

'My seatbelt had jammed. I was hanging upside down. So was Jo, but she…' He paused, seeing the horrific image in his head. 'She had blood trickling down her face…'

Ellie closed her eyes, as if she could feel his hurt and distress. *'Logan…'*

'They got me out first. The firemen. It took

them a lot longer to get her out, and by the time they did she was…' He rubbed at his eyes.

In that moment Ellie got up from her chair and came to sit beside him. She draped her arm around his shoulder.

He sank into her, appreciating her warmth. Her comfort.

'There was nothing to be done for Jo, but she was just past twenty-four weeks pregnant and I thought there might be a chance for our daughter. I had to do it. I had to try and give her a chance at life. Just weeks ago I'd seen her at the scan—heart beating, hiccupping. She was a *person*. She was alive and she deserved to live.'

'What did you do?'

'I told them to do a Caesarean.'

He was aware of her silence as she took in this news. He knew that she might disagree with his actions—knew that some people thought it was the wrong thing to do—but he'd already thought of himself as a father, and he'd lost the mother of his child. He wouldn't lose his baby, too. Not when she had the chance to survive.

'You're so brave…' She slipped her hand into his.

He stared at their interlinked fingers for a moment in disbelief that he was holding her hand again. 'I wasn't brave. I was desperate.'

'You did the right thing. You fought for your child. It's what any parent would choose to do. Isn't that what we see every day, here in this place?'

He nodded, staring into her cloudy blue eyes, and allowed himself a moment to lose himself in them.

CHAPTER FOUR

SITTING THERE PEACEFULLY, looking deeply into his eyes, Ellie felt as if time hadn't passed at all. As if they'd never been apart. As if they'd always been like this. Connected. As one.

He felt so right. Comfortable. Familiar. She had to remind herself that they *had* been apart for many years. And that it seemed his life had not been the pleasure cruise she'd imagined it had, but that he'd faced tragedy. Just as she had.

It would be so easy for her to lean forward and kiss him…

The thought made her start. She couldn't allow that to happen.

She stood up abruptly. 'I'll make you a cup of tea.'

He said nothing.

She felt bad for walking away from him, for creating distance, but she had to remind herself that he wasn't hers any more. He wasn't her boyfriend. She was here as his friend and nothing more, and friends sympathised and friends made cups of tea. It was the British way of things. A cure-all for all ills.

If only it was really a cure-all. We could have tea IVs and everyone would get better.

But it wasn't that simple, was it? It never was. The moment they had just shared was over and she had to push him away again. Unreachable. Untouchable. He was just her mentor. Who had shared his story with her.

What, if anything, could she learn from that? That life threw curveballs? That no matter how hard you worked, no matter how much good you did in life, it could all be taken from you in a moment?

As she poured hot water over the teabags she thought of Samuel. How happy she and Daniel had been that she was pregnant. How everything had been going right for them. The business was good. Their home was coming together, its renovations almost finished.

And then the scan had ripped their happy, ordered world apart...

'Here you go.' She placed the mug into his hands and sat opposite him, taking in a huge, steadying breath. *Focus.*

'I'm sorry. I shouldn't have told you all that. But... But a part of me kept telling me that I *ought* to tell you—because, well, because we're friends still, aren't we?'

She nodded.

'And friends don't keep things from each other.'

'No.'

She thought of Samuel. Had the memory of lying there in that theatre bed as the midwife walked away with him in her arms, never to be seen again. Knowing what they were about to do.

The burden of her own secret weighed heavy in her heart. She wanted to tell him. But this was *his* time. His moment. His sad story. She wasn't about to tell him hers. It would come across as if she were trying to say, *You think that's sad? Well, listen to this!*

Not that he *would* think that, of course, but that was how she'd worry that it would come across.

'I'd like you to meet her.' Logan looked across at her, staring intently into her eyes.

She blinked. 'Rachel?'

He smiled. 'Yes. I think you'd like her.'

Meet his daughter? Wow. That was… Hell, she didn't know how the idea of that made her feel. Meeting his daughter would make them more than mentor and student, wouldn't it?

She'd be getting involved again. Taking huge steps back into his personal life.

'I don't know, Logan…' she said. But the real reason she had doubts was that she wondered if it would hurt too much. The fact that, despite his tragedy, he still had a child and she didn't. Would it be too much? The jealousy? The envy?

It was a silly fear, and she knew it was silly even as she felt it, but it didn't make it any less real. She was happy for him. She *was*. He had someone. He had survived with someone to love and that was *good*.

'You think it will be overstepping the boundaries?'

'No. Yes. I don't… It's just…' She couldn't think how to voice her concerns.

What would it be like to meet her? To see all the choices he had made after leaving Ellie behind? How he had moved on. How he had lived without her. It would be weird. But also it would make them closer again, and although she wanted that very much, she worried about what it would mean for her future.

She had a purpose. A dream she was chasing. If she got dragged into Logan's orbit again would she remain there? Or be able to break away?

'You'd get on, you and Rachel. She's funny.

She's intelligent. The most clever, articulate six-year-old you could ever wish to meet. Plus, she loves talking about medicine, so maybe you two could chat about your studies, or whatever...'

He smiled and...

Oh, my gosh, it's just so hard to say no.

He was trying. Trying to invite her in. Trying to show that she could be more than just his student. Trying to show that the past they'd shared still mattered to him and that he wanted her in his life. That after the six weeks were up in this placement this visit would still connect them.

And a small part of her *wanted* to meet his daughter—the way she would have wanted him to meet Samuel. To see Logan in her.

'Okay.'

He smiled back. 'Good. Okay... Well, I guess the next question is when are you free?'

Ellie shrugged. 'Well, most nights I'm studying, but I suppose I could take a night off. I'm sure my mentor wouldn't mind.'

'Then how about tonight? It's pizza night Chez Riley. Very casual, very relaxed. What's your opinion on having pineapple on pizza?'

'At your house? Oh, right. Well, I guess I don't object—as long as there's ham, too.'

'Good. That's good. Well, what about six

o clock? And I'll introduce you to my biology-focused daughter.'

'Sure.'

He reached into his pocket to pull out a small pad of paper and scribbled something down. 'This is my address.'

She glanced at it. Number seven Cherry Blossom Avenue. It sounded a happy place. The type of address anyone would be thrilled to have.

'I'll be there.'

It was just an ordinary house—Georgian windows, topiaries in pots on either side of the front door. There was a sweeping driveway, but no car. Tall hedges on either side sheltered it from neighbouring eyes.

She stood there for a moment just looking at it. Gazing up at the windows and imagining the life that might be behind them. Logan and Rachel. A father and his daughter. Family.

She'd brought flowers—she'd popped into a florist's on the way there and asked them to make up a quick bouquet. Now she held it in front of her almost like a shield. Why was she so nervous? Why was she so apprehensive about stepping over the front doorstep?

Because it will change everything.

There was a car parked on the road outside

and she used its windows to check her reflection. Typically, there'd been a brief rain shower on her way here and she looked damp, her hair flat against her head. She tried to run her fingers through it to give it a little lift, a little body, but her hair was thick and heavy and it sat on top of her head like a used mop. She let out a frustrated sigh, standing up straight again, and headed towards the front door.

Her right hand hovered over the door-knocker for just a moment, and she had to tell herself quietly that she was being ridiculous. There was nothing to be afraid of here. This was just two friends catching up. That was all.

She knocked. Part of her expected Rachel to answer the door. Wasn't that what children did? Raced to the front door ahead of their parents because it was fun? But it was Logan who answered.

He opened the door, stepping back with a smile and welcoming her in. Seeing him made her heart skip a beat, as it always did.

'Did you find us okay?' He looked awkward, then laughed. 'What am I saying? Of course you did—you're here. Ignore me. I'm just nervous.'

Ellie smiled. 'Snap.' And then she passed him the bouquet. 'These are for you.'

He accepted gracefully. 'They're wonderful. Thank you.'

'No problem.'

'Let me take your coat.'

She shrugged out of it and passed it to him and Logan hung it next to some others. One of which was bright red.

Logan saw her notice it. 'It's her favourite colour—red. Because it's like blood.'

Ellie's eyebrows rose. 'Okay... Well, that's good, because I've got a little something for Rachel too.'

Logan began to explain. 'She's not really one for toys...'

Ellie pulled from her bag the gift, which had been wrapped in coloured paper.

'What is it?'

'You'll have to wait and see,' Ellie said with a smile. 'Where is Rachel? I can't wait to meet her.'

'She's in the sitting room.'

He seemed to have a nice house. From what she could see it was neat and clean. Very minimalist. The walls were a light grey, the skirting boards and frames glossy white. A large mirror in the hall reflected the coat rack and the two pairs of shoes that sat neatly by the front door. One pair big, the other small.

Ellie could hear that the television was on, but when they went into the sitting room she saw that Rachel was not watching children's television, but a documentary about someone who was infected by the leishmaniasis parasite. She turned to look at Logan with an amused smile on her face, and in return he shrugged.

'It's what she likes.'

'Then I think I've got her the right gift.'

Logan bent down to pick up the TV remote and pressed 'pause'. 'Rachel, our guest is here. Remember I told you about Ellie?'

Rachel turned to face her and Ellie was struck by how much she looked like her father. They had the same eyes. Dark and alert, twinkling with intelligence.

'Are you a doctor?'

'Not yet. But I will be one day. Your father is helping me.'

'I am going to be a doctor one day.'

'That's good. That you know what you want to be. I didn't know when *I* was six.'

'Do you have autism?' Rachel asked.

Ellie shook her head. No.

'That's why you didn't know when you were six, then. You didn't have a superpower like me.'

Ellie laughed. 'No. No superpowers for me. But I have brought a gift.'

She held out the wrapped parcel towards Rachel. For a moment she didn't think the young girl would take it, but Rachel looked to her father, who gave her a nod of permission.

Rachel placed the gift on her lap and instead of ripping through the paper carefully sought out where the pieces of the sticky tape were and carefully picked it undone, revealing the human anatomy jigsaw puzzle that had been hidden underneath.

Rachel gaze at it in awe, then beamed a smile at her father. 'Look! You can see all the nerves! The muscles! The bones! They're all labelled!'

Logan nodded, smiling. 'I can see that.' He looked at Ellie. 'You picked the right gift. How did you know you could even get these?'

'You won't believe this, but one of my university lecturers mentioned you could get them as a study aid.'

'It's perfect. Thank you. What do you say, Rachel?'

'Thank you, Ellie.' Rachel immediately got down on the floor, kneeling by the glass coffee table, and tipped out the pieces onto its surface.

'That should keep her busy until dinner. Can I get you a drink?'

She nodded. 'Whatever you're having is fine by me.'

'I've got a pot of coffee. It's usually a permanent fixture in this house. You take it white with one sugar, don't you?'

'You remember?'

'I remember lots of things.'

She sucked in a breath. What else did he remember? How they'd used to lie entwined in each other's bodies? How they'd used to make each other laugh? How they'd used to kiss each other so hard they almost couldn't breathe?

He walked her into the kitchen and grabbed two mugs from a mug tree. He poured in coffee, then milk, added sugar and passed one of the drinks over, indicating that she should sit down so they could talk.

'She looks like you, Logan.'

'You think so?'

'Very much.' She took a sip from her mug. 'You must be very proud of her.'

'I am. I just wish things weren't so hard for her.'

'How so?'

'Not having her mother. I worry that I'm not enough for her. Whether I'll give the right advice. She doesn't have many friends at school.'

'Is she in mainstream?'

He nodded. 'We try to talk about her Asperger's as a positive thing, and it is. I talk about famous people, both past and present, who had the same thing, and what they managed to achieve, so she can see that the whole world is her oyster, but…'

'But?'

'What if it's not? I want her to be happy.'

'She seems content.'

'You've only known her five minutes.'

Ellie nodded. That was true. What did she know about anything? She sat there not knowing what to say. Perhaps this had been a bad idea? She'd almost called to cancel, then realised she didn't have Logan's telephone number. And now she was here, and it was awkward, because she still had deep feelings for this man and though he was less than a metre away they felt so far apart.

'Finished!'

They both turned to look at Rachel, who stood in the doorway smiling.

Ellie was surprised. 'Already? It had a hundred pieces!'

'It was easy. Come look.' And she turned and disappeared.

Logan and Ellie got up to follow and stood in surprise in the sitting room to see the completed jigsaw laid out on the coffee table.

Ellie gaped. 'Wow! That's amazing, Rachel. *You're* amazing.'

Rachel seemed pleased with her praise. 'I told you. I have a superpower.'

She nodded. 'Yes. You certainly do.'

They made the pizza themselves—Logan and Rachel. He'd bought a pre-made base, but they added all the toppings themselves—*passata*, ham, pineapple, green peppers, sweetcorn, cherry tomatoes, mushroom. No cheese.

'You don't like cheese?' Ellie asked them both.

'No. And the base is gluten-free, by the way.'

'Okay. That's fine by me.'

Logan and his daughter had clearly made pizza together before. They worked as a well-oiled team—Logan chopping and prepping as Rachel spread everything out on the pizza base in perfectly organised spirals. She was very precise as to how she placed everything, her little face screwed up in concentration.

'What kind of doctor do you want to be?' Rachel asked her. 'My daddy saves babies.'

'Well, I'm doing that too, at the moment, but I'm hoping to work with transplant teams.'

Rachel nodded. 'Organ donation.'

'That's right.' It felt strange to be having a conversation that was so grown up with a child who was so young, but that was the beauty of autism. It was full of surprises.

'Are *you* an organ donor?' Rachel asked.

'Yes.'

'That's a good thing.'

'Yes.'

Logan smiled at the two of them as he chopped salad, ready to go with the pizza, and Ellie caught his eye. At first she was pleased at his pleasure and then she was afraid of it.

'What type of doctor do *you* want to be when you grow up, Rachel?'

'I don't know yet.'

'Well, you have plenty of time to work that out. Logan, is there anything else I can do to help?'

'Er... We need the table set. Rachel, why don't you show Ellie where everything is and help her?'

And soon they all were quietly busy, preparing for their dinner together, and Ellie found herself looking at Logan and Rachael in moments when they didn't notice, just enjoying the feeling of being part of something.

Was this what it felt like to be a family? She'd never got a chance to experience it with Daniel. It had just been the two of them, and even though they'd started to prepare a nursery for Samuel the decoration had stopped halfway through after that damning diagnosis.

Grief and pain had stopped everything in its

tracks. Not just the decorating, but their relationship, too. Neither of them had known how to talk to the other and they'd spent the rest of their time together existing alongside each other, but not living.

This moment she was sharing with Logan and his daughter was giving her all the good feelings. It felt warm and comforting. Reassuring. *Nice*. They each had a purpose, they each knew their role, and they could rely on each other to get it done. There was a cosy atmosphere, and the smell of the pizza cooking in the oven filled the kitchen with a delicious aroma.

'Smells great,' she said.

Logan peered into the oven. 'Another five minutes, I'd say.'

He looked happy in the kitchen. 'Do you like cooking?' she asked.

He shrugged. 'It never used to be my thing. But Rachel only likes certain foods, so we know what we're going to have each and every day.'

Ellie nodded. She understood that a lot of people who had autism liked order and repetition. It made them feel secure if they knew what was going to happen. It was a feeling she could understand. Everything in life was so uncertain—if you could control some things that firmly, why wouldn't you?

Perhaps I ought to make myself a weekly menu and stick to it? Then there'd be some certainty in my life.

'What drink would everyone like with dinner?'

Ellie filled the glasses. Orange juice for Rachel. Plain water for her and Logan. Then she sat down as he pulled the pizza from the oven and laid it on a wooden board in the centre of the table, before cutting it into slices.

'This looks delicious.'

'Wait till you taste it.' Logan served out the slices and then passed her the salad bowl.

She took a small amount and waited for Logan and Rachel to do the same before she started. Logan was right. It *was* delicious!

Who'd have thought that pizza without cheese could taste so nice?

'So, Ellie, what happened to all those ideas you had of running your own business?' asked Logan.

She dabbed at her mouth with a napkin, giving herself time to pause. This wasn't the moment to mention Samuel. 'I followed them. I had my own coffee shop and book store.'

He looked interested. 'Here in London?'

'Yes.'

'And…do you still have it?'

She looked away, forced a smile. 'No.'

'You gave it up to pursue medicine?'

It seemed the easiest way to get out of explaining. Especially with Rachel at the table. 'Yes.'

'What was it called? I might have been in and not known about it.'

'Stories on the Side. It was in Finsbury Park.'

He looked at her in surprise and awe. 'That's amazing! Couldn't you have kept it going with a trusted manager? So that you'd have an extra income coming in whilst you're training?' He must have seen the look of discomfort on her face, because then he said, 'I'm sorry. I'm prying. I shouldn't do that. It's not my place.'

Ellie smiled. No it wasn't. Not any more. But it was getting harder and harder to remember the need to resist him. 'Do you think you ever went in there?'

Logan seemed to think about it. 'I'm not sure I did. Sorry.'

'That's okay. It was quite small, and it wasn't there for very long.'

'Was it successful?'

'In the time it was there? Yes.'

To start with, anyway. Then Samuel had died and her business had crumbled to nothing.

'And your parents? How are they? Dad still doing okay?'

She nodded. 'He's done brilliantly since the transplant.'

'Your dad had a transplant?' asked Rachel. 'What kind?'

'His heart.'

Rachel seemed to think about this. 'That's the best kind. Getting a new heart. Do you think it means that you would fall in love with all new things that you didn't before?'

Ellie smiled at her. 'I don't know. Some people say that they do. That before a heart operation they didn't like classical music, but then afterwards they suddenly did. It's strange, isn't it?'

'The heart has four chambers.'

'That's right.'

'Here we go…' Logan smiled. 'Get ready for it.'

And off Rachel went on her usual monologue about how the heart worked, the parts of the heart and how it pumped blood.

Ellie gathered from his reaction that this was something he'd sat through many times before and it was an unstoppable description that they just had to let Rachel finish. She was astounded at the little girl's knowledge, and truly believed that if she carried on this way she would very easily become a doctor.

By the time Logan's daughter had finished talking dinner was over and they all helped clear away. Rachel disappeared to her bedroom with her new jigsaw puzzle and left Logan and Ellie alone downstairs to talk.

'Thank you for dinner. It was wonderful,' said Ellie. 'And thank you for opening up your home to me. I thought it might be weird, or difficult, but it hasn't been.'

He nodded. 'Me too. It's odd, isn't it? That with some people, no matter how much time has passed since you saw them last, you can just carry on as if you'd only just parted five minutes before?'

She smiled. 'True.'

'Can I get you another coffee, or tea? Something stronger?'

'Tea will be fine.'

'All right. I won't be a sec.' And he disappeared back into the kitchen.

Ellie took the time to have a proper look at his sitting room, and saw for the first time a picture on the mantelpiece of a woman who just had to be Rachel's mother. She was dressed as a bride. It was a wedding day picture. It was odd to look at it, knowing that at one point in time Ellie had believed *she'd* be the one to marry Logan.

Jo's dress was elegant. Off the shoulder, narrow bodice and a full tulle skirt. Her hair was swept up and off her face and she was smiling shyly at the camera, but looking very happy indeed. Content. It was a look that said, *I know I'm going to be happy for the rest of my life.*

How long had she and Logan been together before the car accident? Just a few years? It had to be. Ellie hoped that she had had some of the happiness she'd believed she was getting. Logan was a good man.

'Tea.' He came in carrying a tray holding a pot and biscuits, hesitating when he saw her standing by the mantelpiece.

Ellie felt awkward, being caught looking at the picture of Jo. 'She was very beautiful.'

He laid the tray down on the coffee table where Rachel had earlier completed her jigsaw. 'Yes.'

'I'm sorry you lost her.'

'I'm sorry, too.'

'Were you happy? Before…?' She had to ask. Curiosity and her need to know were more powerful than anything else.

He sighed. 'Very much so. What about you, Ellie? Have *you* been happy? Has life treated you well?'

Now would be the perfect time to tell him about Samuel. About everything that had happened.

But she could see it in his face. The need to hear that she had been okay without him. And they'd had such a wonderful night so far. She really didn't want to ruin that. She liked this closeness that they'd rediscovered. Why spoil all that when everything was going so well? Besides, she didn't fancy crying her eyes out in front of him as she told her story, and she knew that would happen because she'd never got through Samuel's story without bawling her eyes out.

Was it imperative that he knew? How would it benefit him? It would only make him sad. It would only make him feel sorry for her, and she didn't want his pity.

Tonight she felt that she had got her friend back. Logan Riley. The man she'd once loved. The man she wanted to talk to and spend time with. She didn't want any of that to change. Not when it was all so new. So fragile.

She plastered a broad smile across her face and sat down next to him on the couch. 'It has.'

He looked her in the eyes, as if he were searching to see if she were telling him the truth. But it seemed he'd come to the conclusion that she *was* being truthful and he smiled back. 'Good. I'm glad to hear it.'

His gaze dropped to her mouth before rising back to her eyes. Her own gaze couldn't help but mirror his.

She smiled…

'What's going on?' Ellie looked apprehensive as she saw all the hustle and bustle going on in the small hospital room.

Logan could see she was wondering who all these people were, gathering equipment together, unhooking machines.

'It's Bailey Newport. One of the triplets. St Richard's have got a space in their NICU so we're transporting him over there to join his siblings.'

'Oh, right.'

'I'm going over with the transport. Want to tag along to see how these things are done? But if you want to stay here, I don't mind.'

She seemed to be fighting an internal battle with herself. 'Sure, I'll go with you. It'll be interesting.'

'We're using specialist neonatal transport, so we don't have to take all our gear with us—there are monitors on board.'

She nodded. 'Okay. So St Richard's don't send a team to fetch a patient?'

'No, it's policy here that we accompany our own patients to a new hospital.'

'Is Sam coming with us?' Sam was Bailey's mother.

'Yes, she'll be riding up front.'

'Do I need to do anything? Can I help?'

He looked about them. 'I think we're about done, but you can keep an eye on the monitors on the way down. Any decelerations or changes in the numbers, you flag it straight away. Here's his file. Get familiar with his stats.' He passed it over.

'Are we expecting there to be any issues?' She opened the file and began to flick through.

'Well, Bailey has been stable since his birth, but neonates can surprise you—compensating for ages before suddenly crashing—so I don't want us to be laid-back about this. I consider every neonatal transport high-risk until they're safe and sound in their new hospital.'

'Understood.'

'Be ready to go in five.'

He made sure Bailey's mother had collected all their belongings and helped carry a couple of her bags. When the driver and a nurse were ready to go he notified the registrar that they were off and would be back as soon as they could be.

'Great. I'll get this section cleaned down

and prepped for our next patient,' the registrar replied.

Ellie looked up from Bailey's file. 'We have someone already?'

'Not yet—but it pays to be prepared.'

Logan followed his team down the corridor, down in the lift and out to the bay outside the hospital, where Bailey Newport was latched into position in the back of the neonatal transport.

Ellie stood back as the team connected up the wires and cables and the machinery leapt into life, and as their own equipment was handed back to a porter to return for cleaning before being used again.

He watched her make a note of Bailey's observations, and when he finally got in himself she gave him a thumbs-up. 'We're good to go.'

Logan signalled to the driver. 'All stable here. When you're ready…'

The engine rumbled into life beneath them and the vehicle began to move off.

'How long should it take us to get to St Richard's?'

'Forty minutes. Give or take for traffic.'

They were rocked from side to side as the vehicle went over some speed bumps, and then it was rolling down the hill to the junction that would take them to the ring road.

'Rachel still loves your gift, by the way. I think she completed the jigsaw five or six times before I could get her to go to bed.'

Ellie smiled. 'I almost bought myself one. With more pieces. But then I figured I could revise better from books rather than scratching around for a piece I might lose and driving myself crazy.'

She looked at the monitors and noted down Bailey's stats.

'All good?' He could see that it was, but he wanted her to tell him.

'He's doing well. Perfect patient so far.'

'That's how we like them.'

She smiled at him and he smiled back.

It felt different being at work with her today, after last night. He felt that having invited her into his home to meet his daughter, and after they'd chatted in a relaxed setting, he had somehow removed some of the barriers they'd both had up before. Ellie knew about Jo now, and she and Rachel had got on really well.

He'd known that they would, but actually to watch them interact with each other had been really nice. For so long it had just been him and Rachel every night. He didn't often invite people over from work. He liked to keep his personal life personal. But Ellie was different, wasn't she? And he strongly felt that their working relationship could only improve even more as time went on.

It had felt good to be with Ellie again. He hadn't realised just how much he'd missed her, but now that she was back he ached to spend more time with her. To make her smile. To make her laugh. He wanted to make her happy.

Not that there was any chance of anything romantic going on. Of course not. They were just friends.

He could see through the partition that they were getting onto the motorway now. He checked that Bailey's IV drip was still feeding through at the correct rate, and then he donned a pair of gloves and stood up to use his stethoscope to manually check the baby's heart-rate.

Sam turned in her seat at the front. 'Everything okay?'

'We're good. Just double-checking.'

Sam smiled nervously and turned round again. 'Traffic's heavy.'

Logan sat back in his seat and strapped himself in. 'Chest sounds nice and clear.'

The driver called through. 'Coming up on a traffic jam, guys. Sit tight.'

'Will do.' Logan glanced at Ellie and raised his eyebrows in a way that said, *Typical*. Traffic was always bad, coming this way. But he let out a long sigh and rolled his neck, trying to relax as the vehicle slowly came to a stop. 'Let's take this moment to do a full check on our patient.'

He and Ellie both unclipped themselves from their seats and stood up to monitor Bailey. But before they could check anything they were suddenly and loudly knocked off their feet as the rear of the vehicle came crashing inwards with a screech of metal.

And all they could do was wait for the world to stop.

CHAPTER FIVE

ELLIE WAS THROWN hard into Logan, and both of them slammed into the back of the ambulance, bouncing off the rear doors and then being whacked again in the other direction.

She heard screams, and the whine and groan of metal, then shouts and yelling from outside as a high-pitched sound issued in both her ears.

What the hell had happened?

She felt disorientated, lying in a crumpled heap, face-down on the floor of the ambulance. Everything in her body was trembling with adrenaline and she had to take a moment to do a silent inventory. She could wiggle her toes, move her hands, and she was breathing. Her left shoulder hurt, and something was trickling down her forehead.

She went to touch it and discovered she was bleeding. Terrified, she turned to look up at the incubator. It had been locked into place, and so hadn't moved, but Bailey hadn't been wearing a seatbelt.

She scrambled to her feet, wincing at the pain in her shoulder. Bailey was crying, crumpled up at the bottom of the incubator, and she lifted up its lid to straighten him out and check his limbs, giving him a head-to-toe assessment. Her hands were shaking madly as she checked his skull, his neck, his chest, arms and legs. She found a stethoscope and listened to his chest and abdomen. Remarkably all sounded normal except for his heartbeat, which was a little fast.

'Logan? Logan, are you with me?'

She was aware of him groaning as he got up from the floor beside her.

'How's Bailey?' That was his first question, then she saw him reach out towards her face. 'You're bleeding.'

She pulled away. There was no time for that now. 'I'm fine. Go and check on the others.'

He steadied her hand. 'Let me look at Bailey. You check on Sam and the driver. Then see what the hell happened and if anyone needs help.'

She could hear in his voice that he was just as shaken up by events as she was. Passing him the stethoscope, she grabbed a pair of gloves, put them on and shouted through to the front of the ambulance.

'Sam? Are you okay?'

Sam was unconscious and the driver was clutching his chest. *Heart attack?*

'Tell me what's going on. What do you feel?'

'I'm okay. I just hit the steering wheel. Probably a cracked rib or something. Check the mother.'

'I'll need to climb through to you. The doors are ruined back here. Tell me—is she breathing?'

He looked. 'Yes. I think so.'

'Count her breaths for me, and if you can reach straighten up her airway.' Sam's head had flopped forward, so her chin was on her chest.

Ellie had no idea if what she was doing was right. All she could think of were the basics in emergency first aid. Something she'd learned ages ago, sitting in a drab lecture hall with hundreds of others. She'd made copious notes, and she thought she knew the correct way to do things, but she'd never found herself in this situation before.

'Do you have a phone? Does the radio still work? Call this in. Get police, fire and ambulance.'

The driver nodded. 'Will do.'

With one hand he supported Sam's head, whilst with the other he tried to use his radio to call the accident in.

Ellie couldn't get through the small partition wearing her fleecy jacket so she took it off, wincing at the angle her shoulder had to be in as she somehow managed to squeeze through the gap, falling onto the central console.

She got to her feet and held Sam's head upright. 'Logan, how's the baby?'

'He's doing all right. But we need to get him out of this vehicle. With all this oxygen on board we don't want to be in here if this thing goes up.'

She froze. *Of course*. The ambulance would be carrying oxygen tanks. That was *very bad*. But she didn't have enough hands. She needed to keep Sam's airway open.

Outside she could hear yelling, and someone, somewhere, was crying. Her mind was racing a mile a minute. 'Do we have any cervical collars back there?'

There was a pause, then. 'No. This is neonatal transport, not a traditional ambulance.'

'Damn.' She twisted and turned, trying to look through the windows to see if there was anyone about who could help them. There were people. People clambering from their vehicles, others standing on the roadside, their hands clapped over their mouths in utter shock. One or two were on their phones, hopefully calling for help. At least no one was taking pictures. *Yet*.

Ellie banged on the window to get their attention. 'We need help in here!'

Logan held baby Bailey in his arms and glanced at the small hole Ellie had crawled through to get into the front of the vehicle. If he wanted to get off this ambulance then he would have to fit through it, too. There was no other way off. And he needed the tank of oxygen in front of him so he could keep administering oxygen to his patient.

He knew that ambulances always carried a stock of oxygen tanks in another compartment. There could be three or more full tanks of oxygen elsewhere, just waiting for something terrible to happen.

Technically, because the back of the vehicle had taken the brunt of the impact and the engine was at the front, the likelihood of an explosion was low, but he didn't want to take any chances at all.

He stuck his head through the gap to the driver. 'Hey, I never got your name.'

'Mick.'

'Hi, Mick. I need you to do something for me.'

'Anything.'

'I need you to take the baby. I'll pass him through, and then his oxygen. Support his head. I've wrapped him in blankets, so we shouldn't have to worry about his temperature, but I need you to take him and then get out of this vehicle. I'll follow after you.'

'All right.'

Mick held out his hands for the baby and gently took him in his arms, adjusting his grip until he felt comfortable, and then he took hold of the oxygen tank as that came through, too.

'Now, get out and get as far away from this vehicle as you can. Do you hear me?'

'Yes. But what do I do if there's a problem?'

'I'll be right behind you—don't worry.'

'Okay.' Mick pushed open the driver's door, letting in the sounds of the outside world, and clambered out.

Logan peered at Ellie. 'How's she doing?'

'I'm not sure. There's a crack on the glass here. I think she hit her head pretty hard.' Her voice had a tremor. 'There's blood in her ear canal.'

That wasn't good. 'Is she still breathing?'

'Yes. But her colour isn't good and her heart-rate is dropping.'

Damn. 'I'm coming through.'

He struggled out of his jacket, tossing it behind him, and then began to try and pull himself through the small partition. It was a very tight squeeze. Not meant for him.

He thought at one point that he was going to get stuck, and that he'd have the humiliating experience of needing a fire crew to cut him free, but he finally made it through, tumbling onto the central console the way Ellie had.

'We need to get out of here,' he said.

She looked at him over her shoulder. 'You go. Take care of Bailey. I'll look after his mother.'

There was no way he was leaving her behind. 'This thing could blow up, Ellie. There are oxygen tanks!'

'I can't leave her, Logan! She'll die if I don't maintain her airway.'

He couldn't believe she was going to disobey him! Or that she was willing to risk her life like this! 'And *you* could die if you don't get off this vehicle!'

'I'm *not* leaving!'

'Then let's swap places.'

She shook her head. 'No. You have a child. Rachel's already lost one parent—don't let her lose another! And Bailey needs you. If something goes wrong with him before another ambulance crew gets here he'll need you and your expertise—not me and mine. This way makes sense. We'll be okay. They'll be here soon.'

Her words struck home. Exactly as she'd

intended them to. Ellie always had cut to the chase. And it hurt because it was the truth. He couldn't leave Rachel an orphan. But that didn't make this any easier. His wife had died in a car accident and he'd had to leave her behind, and now here he was being forced to make the same choice with Ellie.

'And what if this thing blows before they get here?'

She gave him a nervous smile. 'Let's hope that it doesn't.'

He stared at her, trying to work her out. What she was doing was either incredibly brave and self-sacrificing or incredibly stupid. He wasn't sure which one he wanted it to be. The idea that he could stand by on the side of the road and watch this ambulance go up in flames was not a pretty one. He'd lost his wife that way. To lose Ellie too would be...

Beside her, he noticed a small fire extinguisher and grabbed it. 'I'm going to drench the electrics and the engine, just in case.'

'Do what you have to—but do it quick.'

He didn't want to leave her, but he knew he had to check on Bailey. 'Stay safe, Ellie.'

She met his gaze. 'You too, Logan.'

He growled with anger at having to leave her, and he had to force himself from the vehicle. When he got out he gave a brief look around.

There was a solid traffic jam up ahead, after a huge HGV had rammed the back of their ambulance. He couldn't see the driver, so he assumed he was okay. A mass of people were beginning to gather, at a loss as to what to do.

'Has anyone got a cervical head collar?' He knew it was a hopeless request, but if they could get Sam out of the ambulance, and therefore Ellie, too, he'd feel a whole lot better about things.

Everyone just looked blankly at him, and he grimaced as he clambered onto the bonnet of a car to see where Mick had headed with the baby. He saw him—a small figure sitting at the roadside on a patch of grass, cuddling his bundle and adjusting the oxygen mask on Bailey's face.

Okay. Logan quickly read the fire extinguisher instructions, then popped the bonnet on the ambulance and sprayed the engine with the foam. He couldn't see any leaking petrol or oil, so that was good, but he didn't want to take any chances.

He gave the vehicle one last agonised look, then tore himself away, shuffling through the people and the cars until he made it to the verge where Mick sat.

'How's he doing?'

'Okay, I think. He cried a little, but he's gone back to sleep.'

'Let me check him.'

And that was when he realised he didn't have his stethoscope, or anything else he would usually rely on. It was all in the ambulance. He glanced back at the vehicle, his anger rising at the fact that this whole thing had happened and that he'd had to leave Ellie behind. He didn't want to tear his gaze away, somehow feeling that if he kept staring at the ambulance then Ellie and Sam would be okay.

But he didn't have any time for anger. Bailey came first. He had to protect his patient.

He laid his ear against Bailey's chest and held his wristwatch in front of his face as he counted heartbeats for ten seconds.

He smiled. Something to feel good about. Bailey was doing well. His rate was the same as it had been before the crash. 'Pass me the baby.'

Mick handed him over. 'I ought to try and get people off the road,' he said. 'Emergency services will be here soon.'

Logan stared at their crumpled vehicle and at the figures he could see hunched in the front of it. Ellie was still holding Sam's airway open with her hands.

'Let's hope so.'

He didn't know what he'd feel if things got

a lot worse than they already were. *Why* was Ellie being so careless with her own life? He didn't know whether to be furious with her or to admire her.

So he chose the latter.

The second Logan left the ambulance Ellie truly felt the full force of her adrenaline. She was holding Sam's airway clear with her hands and arms, as she kept her head upright, and they really began to tremble.

She couldn't quite believe she'd sent him away. But what else could she have done? Left him in the ambulance with Sam? When he was a father to a little girl who needed him? Who would be devastated by the loss of a second parent if anything went wrong?

She hoped and prayed that it wouldn't.

She whispered her prayers out loud. 'Please don't blow up this truck. I'm still in it. And so is this poor woman. And she's a mother, too. To *three* babies! If you're up there, Lord, please look kindly upon us. Haven't we already been through enough?'

Her words must have brought Sam back to semi-consciousness, because her eyes rolled and she began to mutter, her eyelids flickering.

'Sam? Hey, Sam. It's me—Ellie. Remember? We're still on the ambulance. There's been an accident, but you're okay. I just need you to stay still for me.'

'Baby... Bailey...'

'He's all right. He's fine. And we're going to be okay, too. But I need you to hold still. Hold still for me, okay?'

But Sam kept trying to move, pushing at her and waving her arms about. Was she being combative because of her head injury? It must be a closed head injury if that was the case. The blood coming from her ear was the only sign.

Ellie struggled to hold on to her, turning her head away so that she didn't get hit in the face by Sam's flailing arms.

And then she began to hear sirens.

Oh, thank God!

'Help's coming, Sam. They're nearly here.'

The sound of their approach gave Ellie an extra boost of strength and a feeling of confidence that things were all going to be okay. She trusted in the fact that Logan had sprayed the engine with the fire extinguisher, and she felt sure that he would have told her if the truck was dripping petrol. He would have dragged them out kicking and screaming if necessary. But he hadn't. So she was taking that as a good sign. The chance of this thing blowing up was low. It *had* to be.

What had hit them, though? Something big...

It had completely crumpled the back of the ambulance and knocked them flying off their feet.

As the sirens got louder she managed a quick glance out of the side mirrors and saw the ambulance crews in their hi-vis clothing making their way closer, their green bags of equipment hoisted over their shoulders.

Thank God!

'Help's here, Sam. We're going to be okay.'

The paramedics had got Sam out on a back board and loaded her into an ambulance to take her to the very hospital the rest of her family was in—St Richard's.

Ellie had tried to help as much as she could, but eventually she'd realised she was just getting in the way and so she'd stood back and watched, feeling very strange at the turn of events.

She might have died! An HGV had struck the back of their vehicle and by rights they should have been shunted across the motorway into another lane, or crushed beneath its weight. The driver of the HGV had suffered a cardiac arrest and was now on his way to Theatre to have a blockage removed, from what she'd heard.

Now she stood in the hospital corridor, feeling at a loss as to what to do next. Feeling stunned. The enormity of what she'd just survived was sinking in.

'Ellie!'

She turned at the sound of his voice, feeling a rush of relief, a surge of joy in her heart at seeing Logan again, standing there waiting for her. He looked ruffled and stressed, and his hair was going every which way, as if he'd been constantly running his hands through it. She couldn't read his expression, and didn't know whether he was about to tell her off or take her in his arms.

Tears sprang to her eyes. *'Logan!'*

He walked right up to her, his eyes searching hers, looking for…what?

'I don't know whether to shout at you or just hold you.'

He stood right in front of her and she looked up at him, tears falling freely. 'Hold me!' It was what she needed in that moment more than anything else.

He reached out, pulled her in towards him and clasped her tightly, kissing the top of her head, whispering into her hair. 'I don't know what I would have done if I'd have lost you, Ellie Jones.'

She wrapped her arms tight around him, letting her tears sink into his shirt, breathing him in, sinking against him, relishing the familiar form, absorbing him. She'd missed him so much!

'I was so scared...' he whispered into her hair, his protective arms still around her.

'Me, too.'

'Having to leave you in that ambulance...'

She looked up at him. 'We were okay. We were all right.'

'Never have I ever...' He seemed unable to finish what he wanted to say.

Her heart pounded as he raised his hand as if to stroke her face. Then he hesitated, as if she were forbidden, but his gaze dropped to her lips and she whispered his name, and before she knew what was happening he was pulling her close and kissing her! Kissing her as she'd never been kissed before. Her arms went up around his neck and she surprised herself by kissing him back!

Whether it was just relief at still being alive, she didn't know, but she *did* know she needed this. This passion. This life! For so long she'd been trundling along in low gear. Just existing. Not really living. Feeling no highs, no lows. After what had happened with Samuel, and then Daniel, and her business collapsing, she had conditioned herself to be numb. Existing in a state of nothingness.

The accident had been a flare. A wake-up

call. A reminder that she *was* alive. She needed to recognise that fact. Yes, she had put her life at risk, but she'd known it was the right thing to do. Because she hadn't been able leave that mother alone in that ambulance. She had three babies who depended upon her, and she had known they couldn't lose their mother the way Rachel had lost hers.

That sort of devastation changed people. Changed who they were. Who they *could* be. She knew that losing Samuel had changed her, but she'd realised that she still wanted to live. Still wanted to feel and experience life to its fullest. And that meant taking chances. That meant feeling adrenaline. That meant *living*.

She and Logan had loved one another once. And whether the remnants of that love were still there or not they were exactly what each other needed right now. They'd both felt it ever since they'd met up again at the hospital, and it didn't matter that she was in the arms of her mentor right now—because right now he wasn't her mentor. Wasn't her boss. He was just Logan and she had once loved him.

That meant something.

He meant something.

It was as if he had always been in her life and she'd been on hiatus—waiting for him to come back into it. Seeing him in Neonatal Intensive

Care had been a surprise, but it had also been *expected*, in a way. She'd always known he'd come back—it had been just a matter of time before they ran into each other again. Especially with the new career path she had chosen.

They fumbled backwards against the door to an on-call room...pushed it open. The room was empty, not being used, and there was a freshly made bed. He lowered her down upon it, his hands in her hair, on her body, hungry to touch, hungry for her.

It felt good to be in his arms again. It felt so right. This was why it had hurt so much when he had left her to go away to medical school—because she'd felt as if she'd been losing a part of herself.

Only now she was back in his embrace and he felt so good. Tasted so good.

Urgently, they began to peel away each other's clothes, needing to feel the touch of skin upon skin. The contact of body against body. Heat against heat.

'Logan—stop.'

He pulled back, breathless. 'What is it?'

She laughed. 'Lock the door!'

He smiled and stepped out of his trousers and socks, turning the lock on the door before joining her on the bed.

He looked magnificent. Tall and broad and

muscular. Strong. And clearly he wanted her as much as she wanted him right now.

No, not wanted. *Needed.* She needed him. Perhaps she always had? They'd been apart, but maybe it had always been inevitable that they would find one another again.

His lips caressed the softness of the skin at her throat. The gentleness of his kiss mixed with the heat of him and the hardness of his body was a delicious combination, and she gasped as he entered her, urging him on, pulling him towards her, breathing his name.

Oh, how she had missed this!

When they were younger it had been good between them, but this was on a whole other level.

Perhaps it was because of the accident? The need to celebrate being alive after being so close to death? She didn't know. And right there and then she didn't care. All she could think about was the feel of his lips, his hands, his body moving above her. *In* her.

He felt so good. Everything in her was awakening to his touch. Responding to him as she always had. She'd been asleep too long. Her body was singing with happiness and joy as he stroked and licked and kissed, the heat within her building to an exciting crescendo.

She came, crying out as she did so, and his

movements became more urgent as his own climax swiftly followed hers.

Ellie couldn't help it. She smiled, then laughed with relief, holding him to her as he slowed and stilled, his lips against her neck, gently kissing her, before he lifted his head to look into her eyes.

'You always did drive me crazy, Ellie Jones.'

She lay in his arms on the hospital bed and he couldn't help but turn and kiss the top of her head. To have her here with him... Safe, no longer in that ambulance, but *here*, and secure, no longer in danger... She had *no idea* how that made him feel.

She's back where she's always belonged. In my arms.

He'd watched them pull Sam from the ambulance and peered over the heads of the crowd, waiting to see Ellie come pushing through, looking for him. But she hadn't, and he'd begun to fear the worst. Had something happened? Was Ellie somehow still trapped inside?

At St Richard's he had escorted Bailey up to the NICU, informed Sam's husband of what had happened, and then stayed for an update on the other two triplets, feeling that he must stay to continue their care.

Once the team had fully taken over he had

headed down towards A&E, to see if he could locate Ellie—and then he'd found her, just standing in the hospital corridor, looking lost and numb, with three butterfly stitches near her hairline.

His palpable relief at seeing her standing there in one piece, whole and alive, had almost been too much! His feelings for her had come from out of nowhere and then he'd just needed her in his arms. Needed to feel her, to make sure that she really was alive, that she was his Ellie and…

And now they'd made love. It had been such a long time since he had felt such bliss. Such serenity. Felt that everything was right with the world again.

The last time he had lain with her in a bed, staring up at a ceiling, it had been when they were in their late teens. So much had changed—so much had passed in that time—but now the two of them had been… He couldn't think of the right word. It was like returning home.

'This is weird, isn't it?' he said.

Ellie laughed. 'A little.'

'This morning I thought it would be just another day in The Nest. A normal day.'

'Well, that's the thing with life. You never know when it's going to screw with you.'

'You'd have thought it's played with me

enough.' He suffered a brief flashback to Jo's accident. How he'd been dragged, kicking and screaming, away from the vehicle. Then he thought how he'd had to tear himself away today, from that ambulance…

She propped herself up on her elbow and turned to face him, her dark hair sweeping over the broad expanse of his shoulder. She was so beautiful it made his heart ache.

'I'm sorry I made you leave me, Logan. But I *had* to.'

He felt her hair tickle his skin, liking the sensation. Loving the way her face was so near to his, her lips still swollen from his kisses.

'I know.' He stroked her face, tucking her hair behind her ear. 'It didn't make it any easier, though.'

'And Sam's okay?'

'Yes. Concussion, but okay.'

'And Bailey's fine?'

Logan nodded. 'Yes. And he's back with his siblings now, as he should be.'

'That's good. And us…? Where should we be?'

He smiled. 'Probably not in here like this. They'll be expecting us back at Queen's.'

She smiled, nodded, laying her head back against his shoulder. 'Not yet, though. Let's stay here a while longer. It feels so good to be back here with you. It feels *right*. Is that strange?'

So she felt it too?

Suddenly it struck him, as if he'd been hit over the head by a baseball bat, that he was lying here in a bed with *Ellie*. His student. His ex-girlfriend. That he'd stepped over a line that he shouldn't have and jeopardised their professional relationship.

It didn't matter that he'd wanted this for a long time—and, more than that, had allowed himself to *feel* again. To let his love for Ellie flow. To allow all those old emotions he'd held back years ago to be free again. To mean something.

There was so much more at stake now. He had a child. A career he loved. She was at the start of a great new beginning in her own life. Was he risking both their futures? Would he hold her back again? He didn't think he would, but how did he *know*? He'd ruined her life before and it was all so much more complicated now.

'We ought to get moving.' Guilt propelled him out of bed and he began pulling on his trousers, picking up her clothes and passing them to her so that she could get dressed, too.

'Thanks. Are you okay?' she asked.

He fastened his zip, his button. Began to button his shirt. 'Sure.'

She sat on the edge of the bed, holding her shirt against her bare breasts, looking confused, and then her eyes widened as she realised something. 'You're worried that we didn't use protection. It's okay—I'm on the pill.'

He turned to face her. Nodded. 'Are you okay?'

She smiled. 'I'm fine.'

Logan felt the bubble burst. The adrenaline rush was gone and the implications of their actions were beginning to be felt. He needed to get back to the hospital. To his daughter. To his neat and ordered life where nothing ever changed. Where he felt *sure* of everything.

He was very much aware that he'd muddied the waters. He had enough to think about with Rachel. Up to now she'd been his one and only focus in life apart from work.

What he'd just done with Ellie was a grave mistake—no matter how much he'd wanted it. He'd been selfish. Stepped over the line. Gone beyond the boundaries of being a boss. A mentor. He couldn't carry on in that role for her now, could he? But if he asked to have her transferred to someone else it would reflect badly on *her*. It was unfair, but that was the way of things. People would ask questions. And this wasn't her fault. He should be *protecting* her.

Now that they'd slept together, would she want more from him than he could give? Like before? He wasn't sure what he could offer her. Rachel took up so much of his time. As did work. From the very first day he'd sat by his daughter's incubator he'd vowed to put her first in everything. Which would make Ellie second—or third. She didn't deserve to be anyone's second priority. She deserved to be their *first*.

I can't say anything. But I can re-establish our rules. How it must be.

They'd managed it before. He just needed to have stronger willpower, that was all. Do nothing that would throw them back into each other's arms.

He could create distance without hurting her, right?

CHAPTER SIX

THEY GOT A taxi back to their own hospital in complete silence.

Ellie kept looking at Logan, trying to judge his mood, trying to gauge whether speaking about what had just happened would help at all. But she was wary of starting on something private like that, with the taxi driver listening from the front. So she kept quiet, staring out of the window.

Being with Logan had been wonderful. Being in his arms had been more than she could ever have hoped for. They'd both needed it after all they'd been through. Her desire and the need she'd felt to be with him had overridden any worries she'd had beforehand about her education and her future and what getting involved with Logan might mean.

'I think it might be best if you took the rest of the day off,' Logan said as the taxi brought them to a stop outside the hospital, breaking the silence for the first time. 'Take time to recover. Your stitches… You've had a knock.'

'Okay…' She guessed that made sense. She *could* feel a tiny bit of a headache, and some general aches and pains from being thrown around the ambulance.

'We've both been through a lot. It's been a stressful day. It would be unfair of me to expect you to carry on working.'

Unfair because of the accident? Or unfair because they'd slept together and now he was having regrets? His tone seemed to indicate that it was quite clear that what had happened had been a one-off and should never happen again.

'Will you still be my mentor, Logan?'

He looked at her. Uncertain.

'Because I want you to be.' She leaned in. Lowered her voice. 'What happened today shouldn't have any bearing on the future. It was one moment. That's all. It's done now.'

'If that's what you want?'

She smiled at him, to indicate that it was. But a small part of her was disappointed that he was so clearly regretting what had happened between them. She told herself that it didn't matter, because she didn't need this kind of complication either. She had a future to think about. A career in medicine. Did she want to throw it away because of this?

In her unexpectedly free afternoon she took some flowers to Samuel's grave and laid them against his headstone. There was no sign that anyone else had visited. Her old flowers were still there, so she took them away and placed them in the bin, annoyed that Daniel seemed to have forgotten his son. Just because they'd separated, and he'd begun a new life with someone, it didn't mean that he could just forget his child had ever existed.

Daniel had moved on.

Had she?

I think I might have taken a huge step backwards.

Logan sensed rather than saw Ellie come into the room. He felt a tension, a palpability, as he heard the door close quietly behind him and he just *knew* it was her.

He didn't turn around. He continued taping a new naso-gastric tube to his tiny patient's face and then removed the debris, closed the incubator and tossed the trash into the clinical waste bin before washing his hands. He glanced over briefly to see where she was and saw her standing before the baby, one hand against the incubator.

'A new patient?' she asked.

'Twenty-nine weeks.' He hadn't intended to

sound so gruff, but he knew he had. It wasn't because of Ellie. It was the baby. 'Anencephaly. Do you know what that is?'

She looked up at him, her face sad. 'I think I can see what it is.'

'Yeah… Basically it means that the neural tube that should have closed to form the spinal cord and brain hasn't closed properly and the patient is therefore born with most or all the brain tissue missing.'

'You've passed a feeding tube—what's the outlook?'

'It's a fatal condition. Most babies born with it are stillborn, but some can live for hours, days or weeks. This little girl is still alive, and there's no reason why she should starve.'

Ellie almost seemed to back away, as if being so close to a baby who would die soon might somehow affect *her*. He didn't blame her for being taken aback.

'We'll keep her warm and hydrated, do as much as we can. If you're going to find this one tough you can step out.' He almost *wanted* her to step out. Then he could get on with his work without feeling guilty every time he looked at her. He already had a headache after no sleep the previous night.

'Does she have a name?' she asked.

'Ava.'

Ellie nodded, as if it somehow suited the baby. As if it was the *right* name. 'I'll stay.'

He tried not to let out a sigh. 'Okay.'

'What else can we do for her? Can she hear us?'

'Probably not. But it wouldn't hurt if you wanted to talk to her.'

Ellie looked at him. 'I'd like to talk to you.'

He felt his face tighten. 'I've…err…got quite a bit I need to be getting on with.'

She stood in front of him. 'I don't want things to change between us.'

Neither did he. 'Nor do I.'

'But I can already feel you pulling away from me.'

He shook his head. 'I don't want to jeopardise your future.'

'Really? I need us to be *friends*, Logan. Can we be that at least?'

He nodded. 'Always.'

She looked back down to Ava, opened the incubator and reached in to hold the baby's hand, to stroke its fingers. 'Are the parents on their way up?'

He paused. This was the bit he was struggling with. 'They don't want to see her.'

Ellie turned. Shocked. *'What?'*

'They think it would be too upsetting for them.'

'But they can't *do* that! They can't abandon her because they're *scared*!'

He didn't like her raising her voice in the NICU. 'Keep your voice down, Ellie. These babies don't need to hear grown-ups getting stressed. You know we don't get to say how the parents of these babies behave. They deal with it in their own way and we're here for them when they're ready.'

Ellie looked exasperated. 'But…but it's *their baby*. Their *child*. They can't leave her. They're making a terrible mistake!'

'We can't know what they're going through.'

She looked as if she was going to respond. She'd opened her mouth to retaliate. But he held up his hand, silencing her.

'Parents might make choices for their babies that we don't agree with, but it is *their* choice— not ours. We do our part by taking care of our patients for as long as we are able and that is *all* we are required to do. We're not social workers, we're not health visitors, and we're not judges. We're doctors and the babies are our patients— not the parents.'

Tears were in Ellie's eyes. Of anger? Distress? 'But she's going to be all alone…'

'Why don't you stay with her? I'll get on with everything else. You stay here. It'll help me out, knowing you're keeping an eye on her.'

What he didn't say was that it would make him feel better, knowing he had a trusted member of staff with this patient, and also it would give him some breathing space. He was finding it terribly hard to think clearly with her around now that he'd slept with her again. It was as if being in the same room with her made his senses tingle. Made him hyper-alert to her presence. His body craved the touch and the feel of her once again, whilst his brain told him to keep away.

He would pop in every now and again—get Ava's obs, give instructions on how Ellie ought to change her meds or fluids, and then go again.

She nodded. 'I will stay.' She reached for a stool and pulled it up so that she could sit down and still hold little Ava's hand.

He watched her for a moment, admiring her determination in the sight of this hopeless case. It was going to be tough for her. The first death of a patient always was. But perhaps she needed to experience it so that she fully understood this place and what it meant to save the lives of those they *could* save.

At the exit, he turned. 'Ellie...?'

'Yes?'

He wanted to tell her—warn her how much this was going to hurt. But perhaps he didn't need to. She was a grown woman. She *knew* how this was going to end and yet she still wanted to do it. He could admire her for that. And he felt guilty for cutting her off earlier.

'You're doing a good thing.'

'Someone has to.'

'Half-hourly obs. Alert me the second her saturations begin to drop. I don't want you going through this on your own.'

She looked at him with tears in her eyes but said nothing.

Ava lived for ten hours and seventeen minutes with only Ellie at her side. Then Logan and a nurse joined her, and they all sat and waited for the end. When it came, it was as silent as her life. One moment she was breathing—the next she wasn't.

Ellie held her own breath, waiting for Ava's next one. When it didn't come, and the machines announced their continuous tone, indicating asystole, she looked up at Logan, hoping that somehow he could make it not be true.

But Logan simply got up and listened to Ava's chest for a few moments, then silently draped his stethoscope back around his neck and gently closed the incubator. 'We'll need to inform the parents.'

Ellie was angry, felt tears dripping down

her face. 'Why? They didn't care enough to be here!'

'Ellie—'

'What? She lived, Logan! She *lived*! For *hours*. They could have spent that time with her. Instead she had to spend her life with strangers! People she didn't know. Voices she didn't recognise.'

She had begun to cry and she couldn't stop it. She just felt so much rage towards those parents who hadn't made it to the NICU to sit with their dying child. Something she would have given anything to do for Samuel. They had wasted that opportunity and part of her wondered if they'd spend a lifetime full of regret thinking about that decision.

'She wasn't in any pain and she felt the comfort of human touch. Yours, Ellie. *You* gave her that.'

How could he understand? He had his daughter. He'd never felt the loss that she had.

'But was that enough? She should have had skin to skin… She should have had that!'

'She wouldn't have known what it was.'

'How do we *know* that?'

'She didn't have a brain, Ellie! That's how. She didn't have a sensory pathway the way everyone else has. She wouldn't have known.'

'But you fed her so she wouldn't starve. Hunger—that's a sensation.'

Logan stared back at her. 'It was her basic human right. Ellie, I'm sorry you had to see this. It's hard, the first patient death, I know...'

She knew he had no idea of what it was like to lose a child. 'I want to be the one to tell the parents.'

'I can't let you do that.'

'Why? Because I'm too emotional? Because you think that I'll say too much? That I'll accuse them of something?'

He shook his head. 'No. Because it's not protocol for medical students to pass on such news.'

'Maybe I could observe, then?'

'It's not something you want to see. Not until you have to.'

She glared at him. It was as if he was blocking everything she wanted.

'I'm trying to *protect* you, Ellie. Please try and see that.'

Ellie didn't want to see anything. She simply pushed past him and headed for the staff rest room. She needed a moment to think and process and grieve for a little girl she'd barely known.

How many young lives were lost like that? There was no word for a parent who had lost their child. Why *was* that? Was it too terrible to contemplate? Or was it because a simple word would not be enough to describe the devastation and grief that a parent felt and carried with them throughout life?

She wanted to punch a wall. Or throw the mugs across the room. To scream at the top of her voice. To sink to her knees and cry.

How could she understand a world that allowed such cruelty?

Ellie leant back against a wall and slid down to the ground, staring blindly across at the lockers. Tears crept silently from her eyes and she knew she'd never forget the little girl whose hand she had held for such a short time.

Sleep tight, Ava.

Work became quite uncomfortable for Logan after Ava's demise. It was as if the death of the baby had turned Ellie into some kind of robot. Either that or the fact that they'd slept together had changed their dynamic—though she had said, hadn't she, that she wanted to be friends?

He would ask her to do something and she would do it, but there was no conversation, no chat, no expression, and he was worried that maybe Ava's passing had affected her too much.

'Ellie, could I have a quick word?'

Ellie nodded and followed him into his office. He indicated that she should take a seat, which she did, staring down at his desk, not making eye contact.

'How are you doing?'

'Fine.'

He didn't believe her, and he was worried. 'You don't seem fine.'

'In what way?'

'You just seem a little…off.'

'Am I working to your standards?'

He gave a nod.

'Doing everything you ask of me?'

Another nod.

'Then what's the problem?'

'You're terse. Abrupt. You hardly ever crack a smile—'

She smiled then. 'I'm sorry—are you telling me to *smile* more? Don't you realise how terribly patronising that sounds?'

'You're misinterpreting my words.'

'So make them clear for me, then.'

He stared at her. 'Okay. If that's how you want it. Since Ava—since *us*—you've had a different demeanour. You do your work, and you do it capably, but that is it. There is no engagement, there is no enquiry, nor any interest in expanding your learning. You no longer seem fired up by your studies. You do the bare minimum and then you go home.'

She looked at him then. Finally met his gaze. 'Are you failing me on my placement?'

'No. Not at all. But I *am* hoping to light a fire beneath you.' He smiled at her, to show her that he meant his words kindly. 'You need to get your light back, Ellie. You can't let one death defeat you.' He leaned forward, his voice low. 'And you can't let what happened between us change you. I'm trying to tell you like a friend would. *Talk* to me.'

She shook her head. 'It's not about one death.'

It *wasn't* about Ava? 'Then what is it about?'

Were her eyes welling up? What was hurting her? Something he was failing to see? If she didn't tell him, then how could he help her? Because he truly *did* want to soothe her soul. Had he been too abrupt? Had *he* caused this? He didn't want to cause her any pain. He'd done that once already.

'You wouldn't understand,' she said.

'How do you know that?'

'Because you told me no one could if they hadn't gone through it themselves.'

And she got up and left his office, wiping away tears.

Logan stared at the door she'd left open behind her, pondering her words. What did *that* mean? When had he said that? And in what context? If he could remember, it might give him some clue.

She was trying to say she'd been through something that *he* hadn't. But what? He'd been there when Ava died too.

She'd said, *'It's not about* one *death.'*

So who else had died?

What *was* it that he didn't know?

Her alarm woke her. Groaning, she blindly reached out to grab her phone and switch off the irritating noise, then flopped back against her pillow. Normally she woke up before her alarm, but she'd been feeling extra tired these last few days, and what with all the stresses and strains of the last few weeks—ever since the crash, really—she guessed her body just needed some extra time to rest.

She stared up at the ceiling, mentally preparing herself for getting out of bed and thinking of all she had to do before work. Get washed and dressed. Pack a lunch. Clean the kitchen. Have breakfast.

Ugh...breakfast.

Usually she'd have some jam on toast, or a bagel, or some cereal, but the idea of food today was not doing her stomach any favours.

What did I eat last night?

Then she remembered. She'd grabbed a takeaway on the way home. Chinese. Chicken *chow mein* with seaweed and crispy beef. She'd been ravenous and had almost eaten the whole thing.

No wonder I don't fancy breakfast.

Sitting up, she swung her legs out of bed and breathed out a sigh as her stomach gurgled.

I really mustn't eat so late again. It's not good for me.

Ellie got up and washed her face, brushed her teeth. In the mirror she looked a little pale, but what medical student didn't? All the work and then the studying, the late nights poring over textbooks and cramming for the next day, would take its toll on anyone. Especially when they didn't eat very healthily. Plus, it didn't help that she had such dark hair. It made her skin look paler than it normally would, but on the plus side it looked great at Halloween.

Downstairs, she began to brew some coffee and pottered about, clearing away the debris from last night. But by the time the coffee was ready she really didn't fancy it, and ended up pouring herself some orange juice instead. *Much better.* The acidity and sharpness was just what she needed.

She belched loudly, and then listened as her stomach gurgled some more. That didn't sound good. Heading back upstairs, she was about to get dressed when she felt bile rush into the back of her throat and had to bolt for the bathroom.

It soon passed, but she stood there for a moment, worrying that she had food poisoning. Had the chicken been cooked properly last night? She couldn't afford to take any time off. She rummaged through her bathroom cabinet and found some indigestion tablets, took some of those.

She took the bus to work, and when she got out at her stop the fresh air made her feel a lot better. She strode along quite happily, determined that today was going to be a fresh start.

Logan's talk the other day had comforted her a little. He'd *noticed*. Noticed that she was finding everything a bit hard lately. But no more. She couldn't allow what had happened to derail her future. It had already been disrupted enough, and she was doing her best with the options she had left to her.

She couldn't be with Logan. Not like that. He was a distraction. And if she couldn't be a mother then she would damn well make sure she was the best doctor there could be. Helping others, giving all kinds of people—children, babies, grown-ups—the chance to carry on. To live.

Because life was short, and for some it never even got started. She'd been off with everyone lately and he'd raised it with her. She had no doubt that if she had been anyone else she would have had a warning by now. Her friendship with Logan had prevented that. He'd been a friend once and he deserved her to be a friend now, so…maybe an apology? Or an explanation?

At work, she knocked on his office door and waited, but heard nothing. Hesitantly, she opened the door, but his office was empty, so she headed to the staff room, glancing into the wards as she passed them.

He was making coffee in the small kitchenette. Just seeing him made her heart yearn. She stamped down hard on it.

'Logan! Morning! Could I have a quick word with you, please?'

He turned and smiled. 'Of course!' Then he frowned. 'Hey, are you all right? You look incredibly pale.'

'I'm fine! Dodgy takeaway, I think, but I'm powering through.'

When he showed such concern for her wellbeing she had to fight the feelings it produced. Feelings of wanting to fall into his arms once again and let him care for her.

'All right… How can I help?'

'I just want to apologise for my attitude of late. You were absolutely right to call me out on it and I can promise you that from here on in you'll notice a vast improvement.'

Logan smiled. 'Okay. Can I get you a coffee?'

He wafted his full mug in front of her. The scent of it went up her nose and turned her stomach.

'Ooh, no thanks. Do we have any juice?'

'On a health kick?'

She laughed, dipping past him to open the fridge and look inside. There was a purple grape drink, so she had a glass of that.

'There's a surgery first thing that we could observe. Are you up for that?' Logan asked.

Of course she was! And she was glad they'd moved past his concern. Focusing on her studies, on her career, the future—*that* was what she should be thinking about.

'Absolutely! What is it?'

'It's a planned Caesarean section. Thirty-four weeks. The mother has got gestational diabetes and the baby is quite large. It's just not safe for her to continue or to deliver vaginally.'

She nodded, remembering reading about how some babies could have low blood sugar after birth, with possible jaundice or breathing difficulties.

'Has she been given steroids for the baby's lungs?'

'I believe so.'

'Okay. What time is it scheduled for?'

'In thirty minutes.'

'Great. I'll look forward to it.'

He peered at her. 'You sure you're all right?'

Don't look into his eyes. 'Of course!'

He scrubbed alongside Ellie. With her dark hair swept up in the scrubs cap, and her face mainly hidden by the mask, her blue eyes looked very wide and large. She'd always had such expressive eyes. Years ago he'd spent hours just staring into them, and he hated it that he couldn't do that now.

They headed in, and the operating obstetric surgeon, Max, checked that everybody was ready and the patient was comfortable. Her partner sat beside her, gowned up and looking terrified.

'Are we all ready to begin? Charlotte—I'm going to make a start.'

Charlotte nodded nervously.

'Can you feel this? Or this?' The surgeon pinched at her skin with forceps.

Charlotte shook her head. 'No.'

'All right—let's go.'

'Max, is it all right if my medical student steps up for a better view? I don't think she's seen a Caesarean section yet.'

Max nodded. 'Be my guest. What's your name?'

'Ellie Jones.'

'Ah...me and Miss Jones! I've always wanted to say that.'

Ellie turned to look at Logan, smiling behind her mask, and he smiled back. It was good for Ellie to see that it could sometimes be quite relaxed in surgery. Everyone knew what they were doing and everyone had a job. All she had to do was witness it and soak it all in.

'Make sure you ask Max some questions, Ellie. Keep him on his toes.'

Max raised an eyebrow as he worked beneath the theatre lights. 'As you can see, Miss Jones, I am currently making my way through the subcutaneous fat...'

Ellie leaned forward for a better view.

Logan hoped she would make the most of the experience. She'd been really good in surgery before, with the gastroschisis case.

'And now I'm cutting through the rectus sheath. Do you know what that is?'

'Err...no. Sorry.'

'It's the sheath that contains the transverse abdominal, external and internal oblique muscles.'

'Ah...okay.'

Logan heard her clear her throat and glanced

at her as he detected a weird movement. Had she swayed a little? But, staring at her now he thought she seemed as steady as a rock, so perhaps he was fretting unnecessarily?

Besides, he had his own equipment to check and get ready—ready to receive the baby when necessary.

Max continued with his commentary. 'This is the peritoneum, and here you can see the abdominal cavity. Can you see it? Have a good look.'

Ellie bent forward. 'Err...yes.' She gulped.

Logan waited with the paediatrician to receive the baby. They would assess it together, and hopefully it would be all right to go to its mother and stay there. They would check its observations half-hourly, to monitor the blood glucose, but he was hoping for a good outcome.

Ellie could feel sweat beading her forehead. She was beginning to feel a little light-headed and regretted not managing any breakfast that morning. Mind you, she hadn't been expecting to go straight into surgery!

She glanced up to look at Max, the surgeon, who was concentrating hard, and then she glanced at Logan. He was saying something to the paediatrician, checking the equipment again as he waited for the baby to arrive.

Ellie was trying her hardest not to think of the smells and sights assailing her senses. The coppery rich scent of blood, the stink of the cauterising blade as it burnt flesh, the look of the yellow globulous fat and the redness of the blood and the...

She blinked, feeling a little unsteady. Her stomach was beginning to roll.

Panicking, she eyed the door to the scrub room. Could she leave? Would that be bad form? Would it raise questions? She didn't want to get a reputation as a student who couldn't make it through a short surgery. She needed to stay! How long did C-sections take anyway? Thirty minutes? Forty? She could last for that, right?

Just concentrate on something else...

'I'm now about to incise the uterus...'

Logan watched as, almost in slow motion, Ellie swayed violently and then went crashing to the floor, taking with her a tray of instruments.

'Ellie!' He wanted to take care of her, but Max had got the baby out at this point, and he knew it had to be his first priority, so he shouted at a nurse. 'Take care of Ellie! Get her on a trolley and keep me updated!'

The baby was crying. He was large and pink,

lustily using his lungs, and Logan was aware in his peripheral vision that someone was hoisting Ellie up onto a trolley and wheeling her from the theatre.

He didn't have time to worry about her there and then. He needed to assess the baby. But the paediatrician seemed happy with his oxygen and APGAR score.

'I think he can go to Mum.'

'Do you need me?' he asked urgently, fighting the urge to just run from the theatre right now and check on Ellie.

'We'll be okay. Go and check on your student.'

Max turned to look at him. 'Better get one with a stronger stomach, Dr Riley!'

Logan ignored the jibe and went rushing out, pulling off his gloves, mask and gown and tossing them into the trash. Outside in the corridor he saw her, still perched on the trolley bed, looking pale and washed out.

'Ellie! Are you okay?'

She groaned. 'I guess that takeaway isn't doing me any favours... Ugh, I think I'm going to be sick...'

He fetched her a bowl and held it in front of her, but she didn't throw up—which was good. 'Maybe you should go home if you're this ill.'

'No, I'm good... I'm okay. It was just...'

Her face went a little green and he held up the bowl again, but she pushed it away. He smiled, relieved that it seemed to be something simple like a stomach upset and not anything more serious.

'Maybe don't use that takeaway again, huh?'

She managed a pasty, clammy smile and belched. 'Maybe not.'

'Maybe you should have an IV? Get some fluids on board?'

'Maybe... I've not been able to eat anything this morning.'

'Well, there you go, then. That's your issue. Best not to go into surgery with an empty stomach.'

'I'm sorry I embarrassed you in front of your colleagues.'

'You didn't.'

'I bet I did. I'll apologise later.'

'Don't worry about it.' He laid his hand on her arm, rubbed it. 'You just get better.'

She looked up at him with those wide blue eyes of hers—eyes that he would happily wallow in if he could.

'I'll try.'

Ellie was mortified. She had never, ever fainted in surgery before. Hadn't even come close to it! Surgery fascinated her. Seeing someone's insides was like being given a special preview of something magical and fantastic. A hidden world. To pass out like that was embarrassing! She wanted to be a *surgeon*, for crying out loud!

Logan was right. She ought to have tried to eat something before surgery. But she'd felt so rotten earlier, and then nausea had really hit her hard as she'd watched the surgeon cut through those fatty layers…

Ellie groaned, just thinking about it, and lay back against the trolley, feeling a clamminess against her skin. Perhaps she should accept an IV? Because right there and then she didn't imagine she'd be ready to eat for a while.

It was weird, but the last time she'd felt this sick she'd been pregnant with Samuel—but she couldn't be pregnant because she was on the pill. She pulled her phone from her pocket and looked up the efficacy rates of the contraceptive pill. She knew they were pretty high, but right now, when she was feeling this rough, it wouldn't hurt to reassure herself, right?

More than ninety-nine percent effective. Good! She read on. *If taken regularly.* Which she did. Didn't she? Okay, sometimes she'd come home from work and flop right into bed. But she always tried to remember to take it before going to sleep. It hadn't been a huge priority as she hadn't been sleeping with anyone. Perhaps she had missed one…maybe two…

Surely not?

But the possibility that she'd made a mistake kept niggling at her. And the nausea that kept coming in waves made the worrying worse.

She couldn't be. That would be just ridiculous! For her to fall pregnant from just one encounter.

Technically, she was a few days overdue. But she'd never had a regular cycle! That was another advantage of being on the pill. It regulated her cycle and stopped her periods from being so heavy, too! Otherwise some months it could be twenty-eight days long, others over thirty!

There never seemed to be any rhyme or reason to it—it was just the way it was with her. Being a few days late meant nothing! It certainly didn't mean she was pregnant!

I'm reading too much into this. I'm panicking because of Samuel. I'm fine! Of course I'm fine!

But the niggling voice wouldn't go away.

Of course there was an easy way to settle it. *Just take a test.* It would be over in a minute and she'd be able to see with her own eyes just how silly she was being.

Ellie swung her legs over the side of the trolley and stood up gingerly. Maybe her blood pressure was low, because she felt a little dizzy, but she put that down to having just passed out, not for any other reason.

There were bound to be pregnancy test kits in the hospital. All she had to do was find one.

Easy, right?

CHAPTER SEVEN

'SHOULDN'T YOU BE taking it easy?' Logan caught her making her way through The Nest. 'You look really washed out.'

Seeing him froze her into position, but she managed a weak smile. 'I thought I'd get some fresh air.'

'Okay. Want me to come with you? In case you pass out again?'

He genuinely looked concerned, and she wasn't sure how to deal with his concern when all she wanted was to take the test and put her mind at ease. She certainly didn't need the father of her possible child showing her kindness. Not at a time like this, when everything was so uncertain. He had *no idea* of the turmoil battling it out in her mind.

Being pregnant would *not* be good. It would *not* be welcome. She had vowed never to get pregnant again. Not after what had happened to Samuel. The risk that it could happen again was too great even to contemplate…

'No, no. You stay here. You're needed here.' She swallowed. 'The babies need you. Not me. I'm just…' she pointed in the direction of the exit '…going that way. I won't be long, and then I'll be back, good as new.' Another weak smile.

'All right. Try and eat something—it might help.'

She nodded. 'Yes. I will. Yes…'

Why was he looking at her like that? As if he *cared*? As if he was really worried about her? There was no need for that. She wasn't any of his business. At least she hoped not. If she were pregnant, then—

No. Don't even consider it.

She grabbed her jacket from her locker. It was getting cold outside. It would look odd if she said she was going out but didn't take her coat. She used her ID card to go through to Labour and Delivery, nodding a greeting at one of the midwives she vaguely recognised and asking where her equipment cupboard was?

'What can I get you?'

Her cheeks coloured. 'I have a mother in Neonatal. Thinks she might be pregnant and—'

'A mother?' The midwife laughed. 'Isn't it a bit soon for her to be thinking she's pregnant if her child is in Neonatal?'

Ellie blinked, not having thought through her quick lie thoroughly. 'Er...well, yes—you'd think that, but the baby has been in Neonatal for a couple of months and...'

'Ah, I understand. Well, we don't have pregnancy tests on this unit. Women are usually already pregnant by the time they get here! But you could try the Fertility Clinic.'

'Where's that?'

'Down this corridor, through the double doors and it's the first door on your left.'

'Thanks. I just want to put her mind at rest, you know?'

'Sure. She must be pretty stressed, having one in Neonatal and thinking there's another on the way.'

Ellie nodded. 'Stress plays havoc with a woman's cycle. I'm sure she's not, but I said I'd try to help.'

'I hope she gets what she wants.'

Well, what Ellie wanted was to take this test and prove to herself that she wasn't pregnant! But the evidence was beginning to mount up the more she thought about it. A late period, passing out, feeling sick, avoiding coffee, tiredness... And didn't she often need to pee, now that she came to think about it?

It's psychosomatic. I'm imagining things!

The mind was a powerful thing. If you believed something enough you could make yourself feel that way.

She began muttering to herself as she made her way to the Fertility Clinic. Her cheeks were flushed, her heart was pounding and her lightheadedness was not helping matters.

It's the chicken. It's food poisoning. It's got to be. It's got to be!

She felt like a thief, an interloper in the Fertility Clinic. This was a place where women came because they *wanted* to get pregnant, and here she was, walking its halls and praying that she wasn't. She hoped she wasn't leaving behind any bad vibes for anyone else. She wanted to get in and then out again, so she could go and hide in a toilet and reassure herself that all was as it should be.

She found the testing kits and slipped one into her pocket, then slipped out of the clinic again.

This felt weird. Weird and crazy. She'd never thought she'd have to take one of these tests ever again.

She remembered finding out about Samuel. She'd been at home alone. Daniel had already left for work and she'd been about to go too. The book store and coffee shop was doing really well. They'd just been featured in the

Evening Standard as one of *the* most hip and happening places to be seen.

She'd been hoping back then that she *was* pregnant. There'd not been many obvious signs, except for the absence of a period, and when the stick had shown her two blue lines she'd been ecstatic! Scared, but thrilled. Their whole world was about to change.

She'd vowed to work for as long as she could, so she could take a decent amount of maternity leave before returning to the shop, or to do the baby-wearing thing and put her baby in a sling. Would that be possible? She hadn't known. She'd guessed as long as she didn't serve hot drinks it would be safe.

To think that was my greatest concern—hot drinks.

How little she had known...

Ellie slipped into the nearest toilet and closed the cubicle door after her, pulling the test from her pocket and staring at it for a moment.

That little bit of paper was going to tell her everything. Either it would put the world right again or it was about to tip the whole thing upside down.

'Don't be positive...don't be positive...' she whispered as she used the test strip and then laid it on the back of the toilet as she got dressed.

Nervously she picked it up and stared at it, her heart thundering and making her feel as if she was going to pass out again.

Ellie stared at the strip in disbelief. 'Oh.'

Logan was on the phone to a consultant in A&E when he saw Ellie come back onto the neonatal ward. She still looked pale, and there was something weird about the way she was moving. As if she was stunned. Or as if she'd just heard some bad news or something?

His heart immediately ached.

He was really worried about her as he watched her go into the staff room and wondered if he ought to have told her to go home. She was certainly off today. Not her usual self. Things hadn't been right with her for a while. She was definitely withholding something from him and he didn't like it.

He returned his attention to the phone. 'Sure. Yes. I'll come down and talk to her in the next few minutes. What are the complications with her baby?'

'Thank you, Dr Riley. I'm not sure, to be honest. The woman is upset and crying but she says there are issues…'

'Okay. I'll be down as soon as I can.'

He put down the phone and got up to see if Ellie was all right. He really needed to know that she was okay. It was as if his head was muddled. He was being torn between wanting to do his best as a doctor and a teacher, and also just wanting to be with Ellie. Get her to talk to him about what was going on.

There was definitely something, and he hated it that she was dealing with it on her own when he was around to help her. But would he be helping her as a mentor, or something else? He couldn't stop thinking about their time together after the accident. How right she'd felt in his arms.

He could take her with him down to A&E—maybe they could talk along the way? Then she could observe his chat with this prospective new mother who was apparently experiencing contractions at twenty-three weeks.

The consultant had said they didn't seem regular, and they were hopeful they could stop them, but it wouldn't hurt for him to just go down and reassure the woman that they'd always have a room in Neonatal and would be ready for her baby if need be.

Hopefully not. Twenty-three weeks was awfully early to deliver...

He went to the staff room and noticed that Ellie was just standing in the kitchenette, staring at the floor.

'Did it help?'

'Huh?'

'The fresh air? Did it help?'

She looked at him as if he'd just said, *Purple elephants are playing bassoons in space.* As if what he'd said didn't make any sense whatsoever. Either that or she hadn't really heard him, and that was kind of hurtful.

'Er…sort of.'

'Good. Well, we've got a consult down in A&E. If you're up to it, I'd like you to come along.'

She nodded. 'Sure.'

'Are you okay? You seem a little…spacey.'

Ellie blinked and forced a smile. 'I'm fine.'

'All right. Be ready in ten minutes? I've just got to check on the Williams baby first.'

'Okay.'

He decided to trust her. Something was wrong, but he couldn't work out what it was and he had to trust that she would tell him if she needed to. Was it just her illness? Or something else? She still hadn't told him what she'd meant the other day with her cryptic comment about it *not being about one death*. And now she was ill. She had fainted in surgery and she hadn't been right since they'd slept together.

Also—although he wasn't sure—it looked as if she might have been crying. Her eyes looked a little red. But maybe that was tiredness, if she'd been up all night with a dodgy stomach.

Even if he didn't know what was going on, he did trust that Ellie wouldn't put her education or her patients at risk. But at the same time he wanted to scoop her up, carry her out of here, lay her on her bed at home and take care of her. Do what he always should have done.

Be by her side.

He had no doubt that she would prove him right when they went downstairs for the consult. She would spring back to life with a patient in front of her and become the curious, interested, productive Ellie that he knew and loved.

It would be nice to have that Ellie back. He'd missed her. It had been a huge shock to have her walk back into his life like this, but now that she was here, and he'd got used to it, he actually really loved it. It felt as if she was here for *him*. And he liked that. It was his guilty pleasure.

Together they walked down to the lift and he pressed the button for the ground floor. They were alone. 'Are you sure you're okay?' he asked.

She nodded. 'Yes.'

'You seem distracted. Still feeling ill?'

She looked up at him. 'I'm not feeling ill any more. I'm fine. Who are we going to see?'

'A pregnant woman in A&E has come in with some early contractions. Apparently there are already some complications with the pregnancy, but the consultant couldn't get anything more out of her, so we don't have any details. Perhaps you'd like to have a try? She might feel better talking to a woman.'

Ellie nodded. 'Okay. How many weeks is she?'

'Twenty-three.'

She grimaced. 'That's early. No wonder she's scared.'

'I'll do the initial introduction, but then I'd like you to take over and find out what the other issues are, okay?'

He figured that if he threw her in at the deep end to take control of a consult, it might bring back the hard-working, attentive student he recognised.

'Right.'

He reached out, stroked her arm. 'You can do it. I believe in you.'

She managed a weak smile. 'Thanks.'

Mrs Rowena Cook was sitting on a bed in a cubicle, her face pale, tear-stained. She was hooked up to a drip containing some medication that they hoped would stop the contractions.

Logan closed the curtain behind them. 'Mrs

Cook—I'm Dr Riley, I'm a neonatal consultant, and this is Ellie Jones, a third-year medical student. They tell me you've been having some early contractions?'

Rowena nodded and dabbed at her eyes with a tissue. 'Yes...'

Logan turned to look at Ellie, expecting her to continue with the questioning.

She stepped forward. 'How long have you been having contractions?'

'For about three hours.'

'How often?'

'About every twenty minutes.'

Logan nodded. Good. Ellie was doing what he'd expected.

'And how long has each contraction been lasting?'

'About half a minute. They're painful. Crampy. I'm sure they're not Braxton Hicks.'

'Okay. The first doctor who saw you said that you mentioned some complications with your pregnancy. Can you tell me what those are?'

Rowena's eyes filled with tears and she sniffed and dabbed at her eyes again. 'She has ectopia cordis.'

Logan saw Ellie turn to look at him with questioning eyes. She didn't know what it was and he had no time to explain. This was serious.

He stepped forward. 'When was your last scan?'

'Two weeks ago.'

'Okay. We do have the facilities to take care of a baby with her condition, but I'd like to make sure I have the best minds on board in case of an early arrival. Hopefully you won't need us just yet, but I'd like to get you to take a walk around Neonatal when you can—just so you're familiar with everything if you have to come to us. It can be a bit scary. If you'll give me a moment, I'll call a specialist friend of mine and chat through your case with him.'

Rowena nodded and he indicated to Ellie that she should follow him out. They headed towards the A&E doctor who had examined Rowena.

'Ectopia cordis.'

'What *is* that?' asked Ellie.

'It means the baby's heart is either partially or totally outside of the chest.'

'Oh, my God.' She looked sick. 'Can it be fixed?'

'Yes...but it's risky.'

'Is the baby's life at risk?'

Logan looked at her and gave a brief nod. 'I'm afraid so.'

He didn't notice the look on Ellie's face as he began to chat with the A&E doctor, talking over Rowena's case. He had to focus on how he was going to help his patient and her baby.

'Are her contractions slowing at all?' he asked the consultant.

'We think so. Since we started her drip the contractions have gone to more than thirty minutes apart.'

'Let's hope they stop, then. I'd hate for a baby with such a condition to be born at twenty-three weeks. The longer the baby stays in the womb, the better its chances.'

'Logan...'

He looked at Ellie then, and saw her face, and he just *knew* that she needed to talk to him. In private.

He waited for the other doctor to go and then he turned to face her. 'What is it?'

She looked strained. Awkward. 'We need to talk.'

'Okay. We're alone right now. Whatever it is, you need to tell me, Ellie, because—'

'I'm pregnant.' She looked at him with her eyes filling with tears, but he almost couldn't process that—because she'd said she was *pregnant* and that wasn't right. It couldn't be!

'What?'

'I'm pregnant.'

'Pregnant.'

He continued to stare at her, his mind spinning away in all directions as his thoughts bombarded him. She meant pregnant with his baby. But she'd said that she was on the pill. She'd said... He leant back against the wall in shock. He already had a daughter, and he loved her, but autism was a risk. Could he cope with another child with a disability?

'How?'

'I don't know. I might have missed a pill. Maybe two.'

'*How* did you miss taking them?'

'I was exhausted! Or upset! Or... I don't know! I had that bad headache after the accident. I took painkillers but I think I forgot my contraceptive!'

He gently pulled her into a side room. *She was pregnant? With his child? Was this why she'd passed out?* 'When did you find out?'

'About ten minutes ago.'

'And that's why you're so...?' He waved a hand in her general direction and she nodded.

'Yes. I think so.'

He ran his hands through his hair. *Ellie. Pregnant with his baby!* Once upon a time this would have been a dream situation! But now...? Now he couldn't think straight. They had a new patient and the possibility of a very fragile baby coming into the world. He needed to sort that out first. He knew they would have to discuss this later.

Softly, he said, 'We need to get back to work.'

'We need to talk—'

'Later.' He reached up to wipe away a tear that had trickled down her cheek.

'When?'

'Tonight? You could come round to mine. After Rachel's gone to bed? About eight?'

She nodded.

'We'll be okay. We can deal with this. All right?'

He let out a heavy breath and walked back in the direction of A&E, aware that Ellie was following closely behind.

Ellie knocked on his front door lightly, not wanting to be too loud and wake up Rachel. As much as she liked Rachel, she didn't need the little girl to be around for this conversation.

The day had passed in a weird kind of bubble. As if the rest of the world was still carrying on as normal, but she and Logan were pushing forward through the day with this huge news hanging around their necks and only they knew.

She had to tell him everything, right? Why should it be just *her* burden to carry? Besides, she was terrified to go through this alone. *Again.*

No. She needed to tell him. Needed to know if he would support her. If this time it would be different between them.

Logan opened his door and smiled at her. 'Come in.'

'Is Rachel asleep?'

'She should be by now.'

'Good. That's good.'

'Can I get you a drink?'

'Just water, thanks.'

'Okay. Take a seat. I'll just be a minute.'

She sank down onto his sofa. She was about to derail his life completely and he had no idea. He thought her pregnancy was the big news—well, it wasn't. She shivered.

Eventually he came back in with two glasses of water. He set them down on the table in front of them and went to sit on the couch opposite.

'There's something I haven't told you, Logan.'

He stared at her, frowning. 'What else is there?'

'I... I haven't been strictly honest with you. About my past. But you need to know about it. You need to know how things stand.'

'How what things stand? What's going on, Ellie?'

She could hear the fear in his voice and she hated it—because she didn't need fear. She needed strength from him. He'd let her down once and so had Daniel, by walking away when it got too much. Would Logan walk away from her again? Ellie was terrified that he would.

'I got married years ago...to a man called Daniel.'

'You were *married*? What happened?'

'The business we had together was thriving. Everything was going brilliantly—until I got pregnant.'

Logan blinked and stared, his mouth slightly open with shock.

'It seemed a normal pregnancy at first. I didn't get very big, but I put that down to the fact that it was my first and I've always been kind of slight, so...'

She reached for the water and took a sip, aware that he was waiting for the rest of the story. She knew she had to be brave. Even though it was make or break.

'I had a scan and they discovered that the baby—a boy—had bilateral renal agenesis.' She looked at him to gauge the impact of her words.

He closed his eyes as if in pain. 'Ellie...'

'We were told it was fatal. That he wouldn't live after birth and that I should have a termination of the pregnancy.'

He reached for her hand and she looked at their fingers entwined, grateful for his touch.

'What did you do?' he asked.

'We were both very upset. Our perfect world was shattered. Our baby had no kidneys! That was why I was small—he wasn't producing urine, and there was almost no amniotic fluid. Daniel wanted me to go ahead with the termination right away. He didn't see the point in letting the pregnancy continue only for our son to die after birth. He didn't see the point in putting us through that.'

'So you ended it?' His voice was gentle.

She felt her eyes well up, almost as if she were going through it for the first time. 'No.'

Logan frowned.

'I couldn't let him go like that! Like his existence meant nothing! Like he was nobody. Without a burial or anything. I needed to know that Samuel had meant something.'

'Samuel? That was his name?'

She nodded, feeling the tears trickle down her cheeks as she reached into her pocket to pull out Samuel's ultrasound picture and pass it to Logan. She watched as he focused on the picture, his eyes softening.

'Yes. Daniel and I argued. A lot. He disagreed with my decision, but I hoped that I could change his mind when I told him why.'

'What was your decision?'

'To carry Samuel to term so that legally he would be a person and then allow the doctors to use him as a donor. They told me that if he reached a good weight then they could use his corneas and heart valves. I knew I could carry on then—if my baby boy had a purpose and he could save someone else's life.'

'God, Ellie...'

'I got to hold him for a few moments after he was born. He looked perfect. Just asleep, that's all. And then they took him.'

Logan reached for her hand again and squeezed her fingers tight.

'I never wanted to get pregnant again because of the risk of having another baby with renal agenesis.'

'Did you and Daniel get any genetic testing?'

'Daniel wanted nothing to do with us. He didn't come with me to the hospital when I went into labour and I came home alone. He blamed me for being selfish and I blamed him for abandoning me. The marriage didn't last long after that.'

'That's why you decided on medicine?'

'Partly. To be part of a transplant team. To see the end result of what that kind of work does. I need to *see* it, Logan! I need to have hope…to know that my choice was the right one. I need to prove it to myself.'

'Only now you're pregnant. And that complicates everything.'

She nodded. 'And you need to know the risks. I can do this alone, Logan. I've done it once before and I could do it again if I had to. But I would like to think that you will be supporting me, as it's your baby too.'

He looked down at the ground, clearly overwhelmed by all that she'd said. 'I need time to let this sink in, but of course I'll be there for you. Whatever happens. You won't have to go through it alone.'

'Really? I will carry this baby and I will find out if it's okay. If it's not, well… You needed to know. From the very start.'

He breathed out. 'Okay.'

She got up to leave. 'I'll go now. I think I've ruined your evening enough.'

'Ellie.' He stopped her from going, his hand on her arm, and looked deeply into her eyes. 'You could never ruin anything. It's a shock, yes, but we can get through this—you and me. All right?'

She blinked back tears. Nodded.

He couldn't think straight after she'd gone. His mind was going round and round in circles, arguing one way and then the other. Bilateral renal agenesis was fatal. A baby couldn't survive outside the womb without kidneys. Ellie had kept her baby alive through the magic that was the umbilical cord and placenta. They had worked effectively to sustain Samuel.

But Ellie had lost her baby!

He hadn't been able to tell Ellie that it wasn't just the renal agenesis he was worried about. Rachel had autism. Okay, she was high functioning, and he'd been told she would have been autistic whether her mother had been in a dramatic accident or not—but did that mean he carried faulty genes? Ellie had enough on her plate to worry her senseless. Not reminding her of Rachel's diagnosis had simply seemed the right thing to do.

He'd always imagined that it would just be him and Rachel from now on. He hadn't wanted to be part of another relationship. But he didn't want to lose Ellie. Not again. Not now that she was back in his life.

But even if this baby was healthy, what would they do? Parent separately? Would he become one of those part-time fathers who only saw his child on alternate weekends? How would *that* work with Rachel? She liked routine. How would she understand all that was going on? A half-sibling who appeared only once in a blue moon?

Rachel. His heart ached for her and the confusion this would cause. He could already anticipate his exhaustion from her endless questions and the conversations that would go round and round and round as she analysed it all, trying to work it out. What had happened and where she stood in all this.

Would she understand what being a half-sister meant? He could talk to Rachel about the complexities of the human body, but when it came to talking about love and relationships, abstract ideas without form or shape, would she understand those?

He couldn't help but think about Ellie and all that she had gone through. How she had kept this huge thing to herself. All those times he'd asked her if she was all right in The Nest, working with the babies, and all those times she had lied to him and told him she was fine.

How *could* she be fine?

She had lost her son! He had died! No wonder she had gone a little crazy over baby Ava, had been so angry at the parents for not taking the time to see their baby. He could understand her reaction now, because in her eyes she would have loved *any* extra time with her baby.

He tried to imagine her going through such a thing alone. Abandoned. Her husband unable to deal with the thought of his son being used for organ donation. Had Daniel not understood the courage that his wife had had to make such a decision? What sort of man walked away from his wife when she was going through such a thing?

Logan felt a surge of anger, imagining what he might say or do if he ever met Daniel. His fists clenched and his stomach twisted and he had to take a deep breath to calm down.

Ellie had been so brave. And now he'd told her he would be there for her. But how? Hadn't he just derailed the future she saw for herself yet again? He wasn't sure what he and Ellie were to each other any more. He wanted to be there for her…but what about if he lost her? What if they lost this baby?

Could he go through the pain of that kind of loss again?

CHAPTER EIGHT

ELLIE WENT HOME and immediately found herself in Samuel's half-finished room. How long she stood in the doorway she didn't know, but when she realised she needed to do something, rather than just stand there and stare, she realised that her cheeks were wet with tears.

Tears for Samuel. For her marriage. For what had happened with Logan and now this new pregnancy.

A new concern.

A new fear.

She'd told him she was brave enough to do this alone, but *was* she? She'd barely made it through before. Walking out of the hospital with empty arms and a partially deflated belly had been like leaving a piece of her heart behind.

She'd known she'd never be the same again. And then, just days later, just when she'd thought she couldn't cry any more, her milk had come in—for a baby who wasn't around to drink it.

She'd debated expressing it and donating it, but had quickly realised that if she started doing so she wouldn't know when to stop. So she had just endured the pain and the ache and then, treacherously, mastitis had kicked in—as if her body thought she hadn't been punished enough.

And every day she had sat in an empty home, wondering how she was going to get through the future all alone.

But the thing that had sustained her, that had kept her going, had been knowing that Samuel's heart valves had saved a life. That his eyes had allowed another baby to see. It had been the only lifebelt of hope that she'd been able to cling to.

And now another baby grew in her womb. It was tiny, but it was clinging to life, and whilst it did she would do all that she could to help it. She could do nothing else. As terrified as she was, she knew that she had to fight for this child too. It was what a mother did—and in her heart of hearts she *was* a mother! Even if she had no child to hold.

Logan had reassured her somewhat. He'd been kind. Sympathetic. And he had said he would be able to get her through this. He hadn't run from it the way Daniel had. Logan had opened his arms and allowed her to feel safe within them. She felt hope in her heart that he wouldn't let her down like before. Life had changed for him, too.

'I can do this,' she said to the empty room, her gaze falling upon the unconstructed cot. She wondered if she would ever get to build it. If she would ever get to finish painting the walls. If she would ever get to see her baby wearing the Babygros she had bought years ago.

Would it be wrong to put a new baby in Samuel's clothes? She didn't think so. Lots of children got hand-me-downs, didn't they? From their older siblings? It would just be the same thing.

'Maybe I'm thinking too far ahead. I still don't know if you'll be all right,' she said aloud.

Her hand lay protectively against her stomach and she exhaled a heavy breath, wondering if her belly would grow. She guessed that would be a sign, wouldn't it? She hadn't got very big with Samuel due to the lack of amniotic fluid.

There was a full-length mirror on her wardrobe door. Ellie went to her bedroom and stood in front of it, turning to the side, smoothing her hand over the swell of her abdomen. Was it larger than normal? It looked as if it might be.

But what guarantee was that? She knew that if you'd carried a baby before you often got bigger quicker, so...

The one thing her stomach *did* tell her, though, was that she was hungry, so she headed downstairs to the kitchen to grab something to eat.

As she prepped a salad to have with some cold potatoes she had in the fridge, her phone rang.

'Hello?'

'Ellie?'

'Logan!'

It felt good to hear his voice. She was smiling without realising it. But then a darker thought emerged. What was he ringing for? To tell her that he'd changed his mind? That she was on her own again? Her stomach griped painfully.

'I just wanted to check you got home okay,' he said.

'Oh. Right. Yes, I did. Thank you.'

'Great.'

A pause. 'I guess I dropped a bombshell, didn't I?' she asked.

He laughed, but there was no humour in it. 'I haven't stopped thinking about it.'

'You're concerned. You have a right to be.'

'I'm concerned about Rachel in all of this.'

She nodded. Of course. He was a father. 'We

could talk to her. Explain to her what's happening so she understands. She likes human biology, right? She should be okay.'

'I hope so.'

She knew it would be complicated, but they had months to work this out. Months to explore their feelings.

What *were* her feelings towards him? They were tangled. Complicated. She'd loved him before and that love had never quite gone away. Now they were back working together. Had slept together. Conceived a child. And yet he was still her boss. Still her mentor. But he had a pull, a hold on her heart that she couldn't fight.

She wanted to give it wholeheartedly to him. To trust him. To know that he would be there. But she was scared. He'd let her down once before when she'd thought they were strong.

'I'm not Daniel,' Logan said suddenly. 'I'm not walking away from you.'

The reassurance was exactly what she needed. Her knees almost buckled. She hadn't realised how tense she'd become, and now she released her grip on the knife she had in her other hand and laid it down gently upon the work surface.

'Thank you.' Her voice was like the squeak of a tiny mouse as tears leapt unbidden to her eyes. Tears of relief. Tears of happiness. For now, anyway. They still had many mountains to climb. Many rocky paths to traverse.

'But I want to keep this quiet for a while. In case of… Well, you know what I'm talking about.'

He meant the first trimester. They might not even make it through that first hurdle. 'Of course.'

'And we'll need to arrange your thirteen-week scan. That should give us some idea of what's going on.'

'Okay.'

She liked it that he was taking control suddenly. Liked it that he had somehow made up his mind as to which side of the fence he was falling. She clutched the phone, wishing he was there with her right now. Just to hold her in his arms and make her feel safe. Protected.

Loved.

CHAPTER NINE

ELLIE WOKE TO waves of nausea and staggered sleepily towards the bathroom, hoping she wasn't about to throw up all over her bedroom floor. Thankfully she made it, and washed her face afterwards, swilling her mouth out with water and blinking tiredly at her reflection.

I look awful. Where's that glow everyone talks about?

Downstairs, dressed and ready for work, she stared at the contents of her fridge and her cupboards for inspiration. She needed to eat, but what would stay down? There was a packet of plain biscuits, half empty, so she grabbed a couple of those and tentatively ate them. It seemed to help, so then she had a glass of juice and headed on out to work.

She felt apprehensive. Working with Logan would no longer be student and mentor but two adults who had made a baby, and she, at least, was struggling with her feelings.

How would Logan be with her today? She'd dropped an awful lot of information on him yesterday and now he'd had time to sleep on it. Had he changed his mind? Got cold feet? She felt ridiculous, doubting him when he'd said he'd be there for her, but she couldn't help it. And as she got closer to the hospital she found herself mentally preparing for him to have backed away—because that was what she was used to.

'Morning, Ellie!' other staff members called out, and she said hello back.

'You look tired. Late night?' one asked.

'Something like that...' she said.

Logan wasn't in the staff room, and she sat waiting for the team of doctors and nurses on the night shift to arrive and do the hand-over. When they did Logan still hadn't appeared. She tried to push it from her mind, telling herself it didn't mean anything. He might just be delayed in traffic or something. But it was typical that the one person she wanted to see and speak to the most wasn't here.

She made notes on her hand-over sheet and when it was over got up to do her rounds on the patients. To check in, check observations and familiarise herself with everyone's cases.

But it was difficult. Everything she did was overshadowed by worry about the health of the baby inside her womb. About whether Logan was going to bolt. He'd left her once before—he could easily do it again.

Her nausea was coming in waves—much more than she'd ever had with Samuel—and she wondered if it meant that her baby was a girl rather than another boy. She'd heard someone say that the sickness could be different depending on the sex of the baby. It was probably rubbish, though. An old wives' tale.

In her peripheral vision she saw a man walk by and she looked up.

It wasn't him. It was someone else.

'Looking for someone?'

It was Sarah, one of the nurses. Ellie hadn't even noticed that she was in the room.

'Dr Riley.'

'I heard he was in surgery. Some emergency…'

'Right. Okay. I'll catch him when he comes out.'

Ellie felt ridiculous. What had she been expecting? For him to come rushing in first thing to find her? To ask her how she felt today? To place his hand on her abdomen and say *Hello, baby*? It wasn't as if they were *together*. They weren't *a couple*.

This was just so confusing! She'd loved him madly when she was younger and he had walked away to pursue his career, breaking her heart. She had mourned this man, hoping that one day he would come back into her life. And now he had, and they had slept together, and now she was pregnant with his baby.

How was she *supposed* to feel about him? Had her feelings for him ever stopped? But she wasn't eighteen any more. She wasn't a lovesick teenager any more. She'd moved on. So had he.

And yet…

Maybe it was pregnancy hormones playing tricks with her mind. Was she really still seeking that happy-ever-after she'd dreamed of for both of them so many years ago? Logan cared for her. Was being so sensitive. He clearly still had feelings for her, and that was making her feel they might have a chance at a happy future.

But perhaps she was being stupid, hoping for a happy-ever-after, because he hadn't said outright that he wanted to be with her romantically, and she had no idea if this pregnancy would produce a healthy child at the end of it. If she even made it that far, of course.

And, despite what he'd promised, would she ever feel she could truly trust his word? He'd told her once before that he loved her. That she was his world. And then he'd gone to Edinburgh and within months he had ended it.

He'd discarded her like a pair of shoes that no longer fitted.

She'd thought back then that he had loved her, but clearly she'd been wrong. Could she trust her instincts where Logan was concerned? He'd found it so easy to walk away from her. He'd never looked back. Never written. Never called. He'd made a clean break and that had been it. Surely if she'd meant *anything* to him there would have been something?

Ellie washed her hands at the sink, slowly and thoroughly. Taking her time before she had to assess the next baby. As she did so she told herself firmly that she had to remind herself that just because he'd said he would be there for her it did not mean they would be romantically involved. She was pregnant and this was serious. The two of them had to work together to get through this. But it would be co-parenting. That was all.

No point in trying to muddle through romantic feelings, too.

Logan had woken late to find Rachel already downstairs, getting anxious that life wasn't running to schedule. He'd had to handle one major blow-up, then get her to school, and then he'd got caught in traffic. By the time he got to work he felt hassled and stressed.

Last night had given him so much to take in. He knew about bilateral renal agenesis, but he'd found himself researching it on the internet, trying to discover if there was any risk for the new baby that Ellie was carrying.

Poor Ellie, having gone through that alone. What fortitude she must have! Such strength!

He'd never expected this. Not now. Once, maybe. He'd thought they'd always be together—until the realities of being so far away from each other and for so long had made him set her free. It hadn't been easy. His studies had suffered terribly afterwards as he'd fought the pain of her loss.

He'd got through it by telling himself he had done the sensible thing, but now…?

Now he wasn't sure.

He'd wanted her. He could admit that. The moment after the accident when he'd held her again, had lain with her in his arms, had been a dream come true.

Ellie.

His feelings for her were so confusing! He'd never really stopped loving her. Sleeping with her, holding her, loving her again so freely had simply made their situation worse.

He'd *needed* her. They'd both been in an accident which, had it been any worse, might have claimed their lives. It had almost been like a wake-up call. He'd been going through life on auto-pilot. Working. Being Dad. But when had he last been *himself?*

The *real* him, Logan Riley, had craved her, had needed the comfort he had known he would find in her arms, and it had been frantic and magical and oh, so amazing! Yes, the guilt had kicked in afterwards—but was that true guilt or just selfishness?

Ellie had given him everything he'd needed and he had soaked it up like a sponge, hungry for more. Perhaps it was that hunger for more that had made him feel so confused? Because if he asked for more wasn't he putting himself at risk of loving again? *Losing* again? Letting her down by not being good enough?

Getting involved with Ellie could mean losing her. Losing their baby. Was he strong enough for that?

Logan sat at his desk and pondered the situation. If this baby was all right—if it even got past the first trimester—then they would be starting a family together. Another family that would tilt his world on its axis.

And how on earth would he cope with that? Just being in the hospital now made him feel that he wanted to go search her out, ask her how she was feeling. Pull her close. Hold her tight. Protect her.

He wanted to make sure she was looking after herself. Dammit. Stupidly, he even felt as if he wanted to lay his hand on her belly!

They'd had one uncontrollable, passionate, amazing moment in which they had both probably lost their minds, but they could be sensible *now* and make sure that would never happen again. It couldn't. Not until they knew what was happening.

So now he felt as if they were circling each other, testing the water, trying to decide how they should proceed.

Would they ever work that out?

Because he didn't want a future of treading on eggshells.

When it was the end of the day they left together and stood awkwardly by the lift, waiting for it to take them down.

'Did you have a good day today?' he asked.

She noticed as he glanced at her that his gaze dropped to her belly for a brief millisecond, before he coloured and looked away again, stabbing at the lift button in the hope of making it arrive quicker.

'It was good, yes. The lady we saw in A&E the other day came up. They stopped her contractions, but she came for a tour of The Nest anyway.'

'Oh, that's good! The longer babies stay inside, the better.'

He smiled, then looked awkward, obviously considering the situation between them. So much was being unsaid. There was so much they both wanted and needed to say, but they were holding back from one another.

It hadn't been awkward like this between them before. Was this how it was going to be from now on? Because she didn't need him being uncomfortable around her. She needed to know that she could talk to him. That they could talk to each other. After all, they were in this together.

'Logan. Are you having second thoughts about this?'

He quickly turned to look at her, an appalied look upon his face. 'No!'

'Good. Because we need to feel that we're able to be in the same space with each other without it being awkward. If we can't communicate, then how is this going to work?'

The lift pinged its arrival and when the doors slid open there were already three other people inside, so the opportunity for Logan to answer was not there.

They got in and rode the lift in silence.

Ellie could feel tears pricking at her eyes—which wasn't fair, because she felt as if she was being the strong one here, and yet she was going to cry, and everyone assumed that a crying woman was somehow weak. She looked away from everyone, trying to take deep breaths, trying to control her racing thoughts, until the doors pinged open once again and everyone got out.

Logan grabbed her arm and drew her to one side. 'We can talk to one another.'

'You've avoided me all day.'

'I've been in back-to-back surgeries.'

'Couldn't I have been in them *with* you? You're meant to be my teacher, and all day I've done nothing but record observations and change nappies. I want an education as well.'

Logan looked suitably mortified. 'I'm sorry. I didn't think of that—even though you've been on my mind all day. I want to care for you, but I don't know how to *be* with you. What *am* I? Just your mentor? Some guy who might have to co-parent with you? It *feels* like more than that. I *want* more than that. And yet...'

She could hear the yearning in his voice. 'You're all those things and more. We need to find a way to make this work. I've been left on my own too many times!'

'I know. And I'm sorry.' He reached to stroke her hair and then stopped himself.

She wiped away a tear. 'I won't break.'

'That's not what I'm worried about.'

'What *are* you worried about?'

Logan looked uncomfortable. He shuffled his feet, looking around them at all the milling staff and visitors, the odd patient wheeling an IV so they could go outside and smoke. He knew he had to get these words out, because they were killing him inside.

'I'm worried that if I allow myself to love you I could lose you. I could lose the baby, too. And I'm worried that if I start touching you I won't ever want to stop.'

She stared at him, her breath caught in her throat.

The words had just come out. One minute he was staring at her, his heart breaking because he'd upset her, and the next he was telling her he might not be able to stop himself from touching her!

What on earth was going on in his brain?

He made to walk away, his cheeks flushed red, angry with himself for saying such stupid things, for stepping over the line.

She called his name.

'Logan!'

He turned.

'Come to dinner tonight. Just you and me. We need to spend some time alone. Time outside of work, somewhere we won't get interrupted or distracted. Please?'

He could see she meant it sincerely. It was in her eyes. The desire for him to say yes. Perhaps it was a good idea? Though he wasn't sure if he'd be able to find someone to sit with Rachel. Sometimes Mrs Bennett his next-door neighbour could, but it was late notice.

'Err... I could try to get a sitter...'

'I could make my Ellie special?'

He smiled, remembering. 'Spaghetti? I'll be there.'

She touched his arm. 'Thank you.'

It was just a brief touch. A short acknowledgement to show that she understood the hoops he jumped through on a daily basis. A touch to let him know just how much she'd heard him just now.

'What's your address?'

She told him and he noted it down in his mobile.

'Can you be there for around six?'

He nodded and then pulled her close. Embraced her in a warm bear hug. He knew it wasn't easy for her either, and that she was putting herself out on a line here. He needed her to know that he knew that.

He'd been right. He *didn't* want to let go of

her now he'd touched her, but he knew he had to and so he stepped back awkwardly, nodded and began to walk away. He was getting as far away as possible from her as he could—because if he stayed any longer he might do something stupid…like kiss her.

And she wouldn't want that.

Would she?

At a quarter to six her doorbell rang and Ellie almost jumped out of her skin. She'd been checking her reflection in the mirror, wondering if the outfit she'd put on was too…date-ish.

She wanted to feel relaxed. Comfortable in her own home. But this was an important night for her and Logan, and for some reason she felt like she wanted to look beautiful. How often did she get to dress up and go out? *Never*, was the answer. There'd been nothing like that since Samuel.

But in the back of her wardrobe had been this lovely midnight-blue wraparound dress, which felt comfortable around her middle and didn't show off too much cleavage. She'd spent twenty minutes debating whether to wear flats or heels and had then decided on bare feet—so that had meant another ten minutes of painting her toenails and waiting for them to dry.

She'd washed her hair and straightened it, put on a full face of make-up that was designed to make her look 'natural' and then dithered a bit longer on whether dangly earrings were called for or not?

This is crazy. We're just going to be chatting. He'll probably turn up in jeans!

She told herself it wouldn't matter if he did. Because *she* felt like dressing up a bit and why not?

She opened the door with a big smile and butterflies in her belly. 'Logan! Hi, do come on in.'

Logan held a bunch of flowers in his hand and he passed them to her, dropping a peck on her cheek. 'You look lovely.'

She tried not to think about taking his face in her hands and kissing him properly. That wasn't what the evening was about, even if that was her urge.

'These flowers are beautiful. Thank you. I'll put them in a vase in a moment. Why don't we go straight through to the kitchen? I need to get the pasta on.'

Logan closed the front door and she smiled to herself as she headed into the kitchen—because he hadn't turned up in jeans. Logan was smartly dressed too. Dark trousers…white shirt slightly open at the collar. He was freshly shaved but had forgone cologne, knowing that it might upset her newly heightened senses.

Putting the flowers to one side, she washed her hands and added dried pasta to the already bubbling water. The kitchen smelled of garlic, the garlic bread having been in the oven on low for a couple of minutes already.

'Can I get you a drink?'

'Whatever you're having is fine by me,' answered Logan.

She grabbed the flowers again and put them in the sink, then made the drinks and gave the pasta a stir, so it didn't stick to the bottom of the pan. She put a low heat under the pasta sauce.

'This won't be long. Then we could maybe eat in the lounge? There's a small table in there.'

Logan nodded. 'Please tell me you've expanded your repertoire and don't eat pasta *every* night?'

She smiled. 'I can boil an egg now, too.' There was an awkward pause when she didn't know what to say. Then, 'Quick tour?'

'Lead the way.'

Ellie showed him the lounge, then the bathroom, the spare bedroom, and then she hesitated at Samuel's door. She felt her mouth go dry. She'd never shown anyone this room. Not since he'd died.

'This was going to be Samuel's room.' She pushed open the door and stepped in so that he could follow her.

She saw him look around. Noticed him take in the still flat-packed crib leaning sadly against one of the two unpainted walls.

He glanced at her and then walked over to the windowsill, picked up the blue teddy bear that she'd hoped to take with her to the hospital on the day of his birth and put in his bassinet.

It had never made it there.

She'd never felt embarrassed at having left his room this way. It had simply paused in its purpose, the way she had in her life, and it had seemed wrong to take anything away.

Would Logan think she was terribly sad for having left it this way?

'How long ago were you…?' He looked down at her belly.

'It's been four years.'

'I'm sorry. Will this be the new baby's room?'

'Yes. It was always meant to be a nursery.'

He laid the teddy bear back upon the windowsill. 'Perhaps I could help you get it ready? I quite enjoy painting, and I've always enjoyed the puzzle of a flat-pack project.'

He smiled at her and she felt her heart thud loudly in her chest. He wasn't pitying her! Or blaming her for keeping this room as a…a shrine. Although that wasn't the right word, was it?

'You'll get good light in through this window and it's cosy. It will be perfect.'

'Thanks. I'd like that. Very much.'

After that she took him back to the kitchen, forgoing a detour to show him her bedroom. That seemed a little unwise, considering what he'd said when they'd been at work. Considering her feelings for him, too.

It would be so easy to fall back into his arms again. But she still wasn't sure what they were to each other, and she needed clarity before anything else happened. They both did. But he was here now, and that was what counted at the moment.

Back in the kitchen, she gave the pasta a stir. It was nearly done. She checked on the garlic bread and then asked Logan to help her set the table in the lounge.

They worked together quickly, and every time she looked up at him he smiled at her. She felt herself colour. *What was happening?*

Her hand went absently to her stomach.

He saw the movement. 'How do you feel?'

'Sick. Hungry. Tired.'

'That's good!'

'It feels worse than last time. *Does* it get worse with subsequent pregnancies?'

'I think each one is different.'

'I guess I should be thankful it's not hyper-emesis gravidarum.'

He nodded and smiled. 'Have you been in touch with your doctors?'

'I gave them a call. They said I should hear something about the scan in the next couple of weeks. My GP is very good.'

'That's great. I think it's best we try to be positive, don't you?'

She nodded, wishing that she *could* be positive. But she would always hold a piece of her heart back until she knew for sure. She wouldn't be able to be fully happy until she had a healthy, happy baby safely in her arms. That was the dream, wasn't it?

He helped her serve up the food, cutting the garlic bread into slices whilst she served the pasta and the sauce. She was enjoying this domesticity with Logan. It was what might have been. What could yet be.

They sat down together and Ellie realised just how much she had missed this. Eating with someone else. Dining together like they had before. It was so lovely! And the enjoyment of it brought a small tear to her eye.

'Are you all right?' Logan asked.

She laughed. 'I'm fine! Pregnancy hormones!' She swirled her fork in the pasta and smiled at him.

The first scan would tell them so much. If the baby was growing properly. If its tiny heart was beating. Its kidneys intact... She could only hope.

'This is lovely,' said Logan. 'It was always one of my favourites.'

'You used to tell me you loved it back then.'

'You've managed to elevate it a bit.'

'It's just a different sauce.'

Why couldn't she take his compliment? Why was it making her feel so awkward?

They ate in silence for a moment, and then, when she couldn't bear it any more, she put down her fork and looked at him. 'I'm scared, Logan.'

He stared at her for a moment, and then he reached across the table and took her hand. 'I'm here. I'm not going anywhere.'

She nodded in understanding, but the tears were already threatening to fall. 'You loved me once and then you left me. I'm trying to believe you're going to be here for this, but... I'm struggling.'

He squeezed her hand in his. 'I can't go back

and put that right. What's done is done. But I'm going to try and make sure I do this right.'

'Try…?'

He smiled. 'I won't let you down. You need to trust me.'

She wanted to.

She wanted to very much indeed.

CHAPTER TEN

THEY WERE HAVING a lovely evening together. One of the nicest evenings that Logan could remember for a long time.

'Do you remember that time we went on that walk down the canal towpath and you almost fell in the water because you were showing off?' she asked.

Logan laughed, nodding. 'Oh, yes! I was such an idiot. Trying to make you see how cool I was. We hadn't been going out long at that point, had we?'

Ellie shook her head, her eyes alight with mirth.

'I can remember thinking what a good idea it would be to show you that I could balance my way across the lock. Show you that I wasn't scared,' he went on.

'You would have done it effortlessly if it hadn't have been for that goose honking!'

She laughed. It felt good to laugh with her. To reminisce.

'We do stupid things when we're young.'

'I'm not sure we do that many clever things when we're older.'

Logan thought about that and sipped his drink. 'Perhaps not. We're grown-ups, and we work in medicine, and yet we've still managed to have an accidental pregnancy.'

Ellie looked down and away.

'Oh, I didn't mean it was your fault,' he said. 'I just… Forget that, please? It came out wrong.'

She smiled. 'You're forgiven. So, how are we going to play this situation we now find ourselves in?'

He let out a sigh. 'I don't know…'

'We're friends…but I don't know what else we are. Our history together muddies the water.'

'We *are* friends,' he agreed. 'But we're more than friends, too. I don't know how to explain it.'

How could he when he couldn't explain it to himself? He knew what he wanted them to be, but what if he couldn't be what she needed when push came to shove? The last time he'd been with her he'd broken her heart *and* his own. He couldn't be that man again.

'We're both single now. We loved each other once but it didn't work out.'

She looked at him as if she needed him to say something—something that would reassure her that this time it would be different. But how could he know for sure?

'It wasn't because something went wrong with *us*, though. It was geography and timing.'

'And today it's history. So what do we do now? How do we move this further? Take it one day at a time? See where it leads us?'

At least she had the bravery to ask the question outright. To ask if they were going to try to be a couple again.

'Are you saying you want us to be together?' Logan asked, hoping beyond hope that she *was* saying that. That she wanted that.

But how scary would that be? Because then he'd have to totally step up and give her his heart—which he wanted to do! Of course he did! But he also wanted to move with caution this time, so as not to get it wrong.

He looked at Ellie and was suddenly struck by the warmth in her eyes. She cared about him. He could see that.

'I don't know.'

His gaze dropped to her belly and he wondered what secrets were contained within and whether their baby would live to see the brightness of the day.

The baby was a mystery. One that terrified

him. Nowadays he and Ellie had modern technology to help guide them, let them know what they should do. But that first ultrasound was weeks away yet.

What if their baby *did* have bilateral renal agenesis? What then? Would he be strong enough, supportive enough to be with her if she carried on with the pregnancy? Knowing what grief awaited them both?

I don't know. I want to be.

It was too hard a decision to make just yet. He needed certainty. He needed to know the answers that would be provided by the ultrasound scan—because if everything was all right with the baby then he could tell Ellie just how much she meant to him.

Perhaps it would be better if he didn't think too much about the pregnancy in case disappointment and upset awaited him?

Logan looked directly into Ellie's eyes and could see how apprehensive she was. Already she was pinning all her hopes on this new pregnancy, hoping beyond hope that this time the baby would be all right and she could finally bring it home to that half-finished nursery down the hall.

What if she didn't? To lose a second child would break her in two—and what would it do to *them*? That was what scared him. Would she blame him? Would he lose her? Because he already had a family would she find it unbearable that she couldn't have one? Could he bear to lose her twice in one lifetime?

Loving Ellie would either bring him utter joy or total heartbreak.

'I've had a lovely evening, Ellie. Thank you. I think we needed this.'

She nodded. 'Me too. I had fun.'

'You should come to us next time. Or maybe we could go for a walk? Rachel likes the park.'

Ellie could imagine. 'I'd like that.'

'Small steps whilst we figure this thing out?'

'Yes.'

She was glad that he was still sorting out this situation between them. It was a difficult line to walk, with so many added complications.

'And of course I'll let you know when I get sent my scan date, so we can both put it in our diaries. You *will* come to the scan, won't you?'

Please say that you will. She couldn't bear the idea of going alone and hearing any bad news by herself.

He nodded. 'Of course. Well… I'd best be going.' He stood up. 'Can I use your bathroom before I go?'

'Sure.'

She watched him go and realised as he walked away that she really liked having them here. She knew that when he was gone the flat would seem terribly empty and lifeless.

Ellie looked down at her belly and caressed it. A new future might be growing inside her. A new hope. Someone who would make them incredibly happy or grief-stricken once again. In a way, it was the same thing for her and Logan. If they gave each other a chance, tried again, it could go right. But it might also go oh, so wrong.

He came back from the bathroom and grabbed his jacket. 'Thanks again, Ellie. It's been a good night.'

'I'll walk you out to your car.'

She tried not to feel sad. Tried not to feel as if she was letting him slip away as he opened the front door to leave her. Tried to feel optimistic that she would see him again soon at work. That this wasn't a permanent goodbye, just *au revoir*.

He turned in the doorway.

Ellie looked up into his eyes and felt a burning desire rush through her. A need so raw and simple for this man before her that she almost couldn't breathe.

She saw his gaze drop to her mouth and suddenly he was moving towards her, closing the gap between them hesitantly, uncertain, but doing it anyway.

Because neither of them could fight it.

And his lips met hers.

This kiss was different from the one when they'd thrown themselves at each other in the hospital. That kiss had been full of desperate passion and desire and an *I must have you now* adrenaline boost.

This kiss was gentle and tentative. Slow and measured. And she felt its warmth and the slow spread of it through her body as she was awakened to the desires within her.

This kiss took her breath.

And then he broke it off suddenly and stepped away. 'I'd…er…better go. Early start.'

She nodded, trying to smile. 'Of course.'

But her lips were still burning from his touch, her body was screaming to be touched too, and her blood was pounding its way through her veins.

Her fingers touched her lips as he got into his car and started the engine, and then her hand was at her throat as she realised what it might mean.

Were they getting back together?

So many questions. And this evening hadn't answered any of them. It had only created more.

Logan drove away, lifting his hand to wave before he went out of sight.

But that kiss… *Boy, that was something!*

She smiled to herself, biting her bottom lip, and turned to hurry indoors.

Logan could have kicked himself for kissing her.

I was supposed to be keeping my distance! It was meant to be a peck on the cheek. A thank-you!

But he'd been staring into those blue eyes of hers and he didn't know what had happened. Maybe it was the fact that they'd been talking about their relationship, how close they were to being together again...

He'd spent the whole night being sensible and keeping his distance, and yet there was a piece of him growing inside her—*their baby*—and he'd suddenly been overwhelmed by a feeling of such closeness and intimacy and love for her. He'd wanted to kiss her and he hadn't been able to stop himself.

And she'd kissed him back. That was the scariest thing. As if she'd *wanted* him to kiss her and she was enjoying it.

But, as he kept telling himself, they weren't together. They were just two people who'd made a baby by accident. That was all, right? So what was with all these feelings he was experiencing? Washing over him like waves? When he was with her he couldn't stop looking at her, and when they were apart his thoughts were of her.

It's probably just because of the baby.

Ellie had so much to worry about right now. She had to be in turmoil. He needed to give her some space until they were through it. Give her fewer complications to worry about.

This pregnancy could be a second chance for both him *and* Ellie, but the best thing he could do now would be to support her as a friend. By creating some emotional distance for himself he would be better able to protect her if it all went wrong. By loving her, letting himself get close, he'd risk devastation for them both, and she would need someone strong to lean on.

The pain he felt, knowing he had to hold back, was as raw as the pain he'd felt upon seeing his newborn daughter in Special Care—not knowing if she would survive. Not knowing if he should love her as much as he did because of how much it would hurt if he lost her. It was like a weight upon his chest. A cold lump of fear in his gut.

Can I hold myself back from her again?

He told himself—firmly this time—that he needed to begin distancing himself properly. If only to protect and support her heart if it all went wrong.

* * *

Despite the morning sickness Ellie woke up feeling bright and optimistic. She had a packet of biscuits at the side of her bed and she nibbled on those to get the nausea under control before she got up and headed downstairs.

Coffee and tea were still off the menu, so she poured herself a glass of apple juice and grabbed a breakfast bar for the trip into work. She'd discovered that if she ate little and often it seemed to help the most. Getting hungry was a big no-no.

But for some reason the sickness seemed a bit easier to handle today. It wasn't because it was actually any less—it still had the capacity to bring her to her knees if she let it—it was more that she herself felt stronger, and she put a lot of that down to the fact that Logan had kissed her. So gently. So tenderly. And with such devotion that she'd felt he cared. That she wasn't doing this alone.

She'd got so used to just relying upon herself, because it was safer that way, but this new way of living felt good, and she remembered now how it felt to know that she had someone she could lean on.

Logan.

Who'd have thought it? That after all these years they would reconnect in such a way and have a baby together. Perhaps it had always been meant to be? Perhaps they'd both needed to go off in different directions in life in order to truly appreciate what they had now?

Once she got to work she clipped on her ID card and headed to the hand-over session.

Logan was already there, and she smiled at him and said good morning as she came in. He didn't really react, but she put it down to the fact that he was deep in discussion with another colleague. And she couldn't sit next to him because all the seats were taken.

She sat and listened and then, fully cognisant of what was going on in the department, got up to start her shift. She waited for Logan to be free.

'Hi.' She smiled at him.

'Hey.'

'What are you going to have me do today?' She was feeling optimistic.

'Well, I guess later we'll need to catch up on your placement file—make sure it's all up to date and see if there are any procedures or elements of patient care you haven't done yet.'

'I haven't followed a baby through to being discharged out of The Nest. Either to home or to Paediatrics. I know that.'

He nodded. 'Okay. The Carling baby is due

to be discharged today—once we've done the car seat test.'

'The car seat test?'

'We put the baby in a car seat and leave it in for thirty minutes, to make sure their oxygen saturations stay at high levels.'

'Oh, okay.'

'Maybe you could be in charge of that, and then I can show you how to discharge a patient?'

'All right.'

He smiled to indicate that their conversation was over and then walked away from her, heading towards his office. She figured he was always busy at the hand-over of shift and must have a lot to do—unlike her. She had an easier workload.

She went to take a set of observations on baby Marcus Carling, so she'd have a base set of numbers before she had to do the car seat test.

His parents were already there, with the car seat they'd been asked to bring in, and she smiled at them both. 'Morning, Jess... David. How are you today?'

Jess smiled nervously. 'Anxious.'

'About the test?'

'That and taking him home.'

She stroked Jess's arm. 'That's the best part.'

'*And* the most terrifying. We won't have all of you guys looking after him…making sure he's okay.'

'But you have to comfort yourself with the fact that since he came into The Nest his oxygen levels haven't dropped the way they did after birth.'

Marcus had been born at thirty-six weeks. He'd been blue, with the cord wrapped three times around his neck, but they'd managed to revive him and get him breathing. Then, about an hour after birth, he'd begun to look hypoxic and his parents had pressed the emergency buzzer in a panic.

Since then baby Marcus had been monitored for three days in The Nest and his oxygen saturations had been fine—not even dropping when he had his feeds. He was looking good and it was safe for him to go home. The car seat test *had* to go well.

'We've bought an oxygen monitor, just in case. You probably think we're being over-cautious, maybe paranoid, but—'

'I don't think that at all. I think it's a sensible step for you to take.'

'It will make us feel safer,' David said. 'What with us both being first-time parents.'

Ellie nodded. 'Of course. Let's see how he's

doing first, and then we'll get him into the car seat—okay?'

'For thirty minutes?' Jess asked.

'Yes. If he manages that without dropping his levels—we'll have a monitor on him at all times—then he can go home.'

She began to take her readings, assessing him for colour and form, tone and alertness. Compared to some of the other babies in The Nest Marcus looked sturdy and healthy. As if he shouldn't be there at all.

'Do you have kids?' asked Jess.

'I have a son.' It had just slipped out, and she blinked hard, realising what she'd admitted for the first time.

'How old is he?'

She smiled, pulling her stethoscope from inside her ears. 'He's still a baby.' It hurt to tell this half-truth, but she couldn't show it.

'So you know how scary it is to take a baby home for the first time? Any tips you can share?'

Ellie hoped she wouldn't cry. Her emotions were all over the place right now. 'Sleep when they sleep. Rest as much as you can. Eat well.'

'Sounds doable,' said David.

She smiled, knowing that she'd never got the chance to do any of those things. Would she this time? Was this baby going to make it?

'Okay, shall we start the car seat test?'

David nodded and got the seat ready, placing it on the floor and preparing the safety straps, pulling them out to wrap around Marcus.

'Okay, Mum, when you're ready?' Ellie stepped back, holding the monitor she would wrap around Marcus's toe.

Jess knelt down, kissing Marcus on the forehead, before placing him in the seat, adjusting his arms and legs through the straps and clicking the safety buckle.

'You gotta ace this—you hear me?' she whispered, then stood up and wrapped her arms around her husband.

Ellie attached the monitor and checked the read-out. All looked good.

She sat back and waited.

Logan observed her from his office. She didn't see him. She was too busy talking to the Carlings. He guessed the car seat test had gone well, because it looked as if it was smiles all round, and Jess Carling was beaming, having scooped up baby Marcus into her arms.

He was smiling a little himself. It always made him pleased when parents could finally take their baby home. It meant that everything was right with the world and all was as it should be. Babies should be with their parents—not trapped on a hospital ward.

Had he now created a situation in which he and Ellie would be sitting anxiously by a cot?

He blamed himself. He'd caused this by giving in to his desires. Kissing her. Sleeping with her.

What on earth was I playing at? I should have been her mentor and protected her. Put her feelings first.

He'd told her he would be there for her and he would. But he also had to remember that he had Rachel to think about. He couldn't start a relationship with Ellie when they didn't know how this pregnancy would go, and it would be the wrong thing to do to get involved just because of it.

What did it even *mean*, anyway? It was proof that they'd slept together, but it wasn't physical evidence that they'd have a fool-proof romantic future!

He couldn't deny that he loved Ellie. He probably always would. But he couldn't be involved with her romantically just yet. That wasn't what she needed. She needed him to be strong. There were so many hurdles they had to get over first—before he could allow himself to think of anything else.

She said she'd do the same thing again if she knew their baby wouldn't survive.

He really hoped that neither of them would have to face that possibility. To watch her go through that would tear him apart. And to experience it himself...? Well, he had no idea how he'd feel, but he *did* know how he'd felt when he'd not known if Rachel would live. That had been horrendous.

And although she'd said she was strong enough to do it...*he* wasn't.

Ellie waved off the Carlings, feeling happy tears prick at the backs of her eyes as she watched them walk away with baby Marcus in his car seat. They were going home with their baby, which was exactly as it should be.

She was happy for them. She *was*. But she was also envious, not knowing if she would ever experience the same thrill for herself. She could hardly imagine how it must feel, but she supposed it must feel wondrous. You'd feel ecstatic and nervous and exhausted all at the same time!

'He made it, then?'

She turned to smile at Logan, glad that he was there with her to see it happen. 'Yes, he did brilliantly.'

'Are you crying?'

She laughed, a little embarrassed. What could she do with these hormones running rampant? 'Maybe a little.'

She felt a need for his arms around her at that moment. Just a little something to show that he cared. So she moved to wrap her arms around him, going up on tiptoe to give him a kiss.

He stepped away, looking awkward, looking up and down the corridor to make sure they were alone. 'What are you *doing*?'

Confused, Ellie looked up at him, not sure what was going on. 'I was just going to...to kiss you.'

'I don't think we should do that here. I'm sorry if I've given you the wrong messages, or the wrong impression of what's happening between us, but we shouldn't be doing this. Not really. *Slowly*, we said.'

His words, and his physical retreat from her, hit her like a sledgehammer. 'What do you mean? I thought we'd had a lovely night last night? We *kissed*! It was...it was the most wonderful thing I—'

'It was a mistake. I should never have done it and I apologise.'

'*What?*' Surely what he was saying couldn't be true? He'd kissed her last night! And that kiss hadn't been a goodbye kiss between friends, or a peck on the cheek. It had been deep and sensual and it had *meant* something!

'I'm here for you, Ellie, but…'

She held up her hand, stopping him from speaking. The tears were falling freely now. 'I should have guessed. I mean, you've done this sort of thing before. I should have known. You have a track record, don't you? Of letting me down?'

He shook his head. *'Ellie—'*

'Please—don't. I just can't believe you'd do this to me again!' And she pushed by him, running to the toilets so she could break her heart in private.

What a fool she had been! To think that just because he'd kissed her, just because they were having a baby, they were more than friends.

I've embarrassed myself!

And, worse, she had done so at work! Where she was supposed to be making a future for herself. He was her mentor—how the hell was she supposed to learn anything from him *now*, without there being an atmosphere?

I can't stay here. I can't look him in the eye. Not today.

She wiped her eyes with tissue and then left the safety of the bathroom and headed to the staff room.

One of the nurses was in there. 'Hi. I'm just

making a cup of tea for a mum. Want one?'
The nurse did a double-take. 'Hey, are you all
right?'

'No. I don't feel well. I'm going home.'

'Have you told Dr Riley?'

'No. If he asks can you tell him that I've gone
and that it's probably best if he doesn't call.'

The nurse looked confused. 'Er...okay...'

Ellie grabbed everything from her locker
and raced from the department, hoping she
wouldn't meet Logan on her way out. She didn't
want to see him. He'd made everything quite
clear.

She'd been a fool not to see it before. His
hesitation. His uncertainty. He'd been having
doubts but had been too afraid to tell her! Daniel had walked away and now Logan was doing
it too. *Again!* They were apart. Not a couple,
as she'd hoped they were. And now, no matter what happened to this baby she had in her
belly, she was going to have to do it alone—as
she'd suspected.

How could he do this to me?

Logan was frustrated that she hadn't let him explain. But to let her kiss him? At *work*? It was
the one thing he wanted to do more than anything, but how could he let it happen when he
was trying so hard to keep her at arms' length

until he knew what was happening with the baby, so he could support them?

He loved her! Deeply. She couldn't possibly understand how much! He did, and it was hurting him to push her away, but he was doing it so he could protect her heart. Support her if the worst happened.

Because if there was something wrong with this baby he'd need to be able to deal with it, and his feelings, without having to worry about letting Ellie down. If they lost this baby he'd be a basket case. It would tear him in two. But Ellie would need someone strong around her.

He'd kissed her last night and he shouldn't have. But his friendship with her, his feelings for her, had kept dragging him back, and he'd needed the connection he'd felt with her. He'd thoroughly enjoyed last night, but he knew he'd enjoyed it too much, knew that when he was with her he couldn't stop himself from gazing at her face, from being mesmerised by her lips, by the feelings he felt within his own body whenever she was near.

Physically, his body betrayed him. Emotionally...? He didn't want to think about that. Right now he wanted to focus on the anger he felt with himself. If he focused on that, then he wouldn't have to think about how her large blue eyes had welled up with tears and how she'd run away from him.

He knew this was all his fault.

Focus on that!

He threw himself into his work, only discovering some time later that Ellie had gone home. 'Feeling ill', the nurse said, but it was clear from the nurse's face that she suspected it might be for some other reason.

'She said best not to call her.' The nurse raised an eyebrow.

'Right. Thank you.'

His duties done for now, he headed into his office and closed the door, sinking down into his seat and holding his head in his hands. He'd screwed up royally. He knew that. He'd led her to think one thing and then pulled away when she'd tried to make things more serious, more official between them by going in for a kiss.

He groaned, telling himself it had still been the right thing to do.

For all of them.

He had to believe that.

She would thank him when the time came.

CHAPTER ELEVEN

SHE FELT SICK. Awful. Ever since she'd left the hospital she'd felt as if the whole world had become much darker. She kept forcing herself to eat, even though she didn't want to, knowing that she had to, that otherwise she'd start being sick. Eating was the only thing keeping it at bay.

And she had a shift this morning.

How was she going to be able to work with him? After all he'd put her through?

Okay, maybe she'd read more into it than she should have, but they'd slept together, made a baby. He'd kissed her just a couple of nights ago and it had been the most wonderful, tender, loving kiss she had ever experienced! Of *course* she'd read something into that. Who wouldn't? She'd felt that their kiss had said, *I want you. I care for you. I need you. You mean something to me.*

And she'd allowed those feelings in.

It meant more than being friends, a kiss like that. There'd been meaning in it. They'd been getting to know each other again outside of work. She'd met his daughter. They'd been rekindling their relationship of old, making it into something newer, something better—something that spoke of hope and redemption and possibility.

And love?

She'd be lying if she said she didn't love him. She had *always* loved Logan Riley. She'd just been very good at hiding it, that was all. But that kiss had opened the floodgates and all those repressed feelings she'd stamped down over the years so that she could move on with her life had come rushing back. She'd been hopeless to fight them.

She'd believed that he would be with her for one of the most stressful events of her life... finding out about this baby... And now?

He'd made it quite clear that they were *not* a couple. That they were *not* together. He hadn't minced his words and they had torn her heart asunder. If she lost this baby because of the grief of that she would never forgive him.

Gritting her teeth, she buzzed through to The Nest and walked down the long corridor towards the staff room. He would be in there.

There would be questions from everyone else. Did she feel okay? Was she better?

Would he look at her? Talk to her? Say hello? Ellie didn't know how she would feel about that. Whether she was ready to see him, or whether just looking at him would make her burst into tears all over again.

She'd hardly slept. She'd lain awake all night, staring at the ceiling, her hand resting on her belly which she could swear was definitely already bigger.

There was a roundness to it—a definite swell. She thought that was good. She hadn't got big with Samuel because there had been no amniotic fluid. But she was also worried that this size increase meant something bad— because surely it was too soon to be getting bigger?

At about two in the morning she'd started searching on the internet for what it could mean.

Polyhydramnios was one thing. An excess of amniotic fluid seen only in about one percent of pregnancies. But that didn't mean anything. Bilateral renal agenesis wasn't exactly common, and her son had had that.

Multiple pregnancy? She doubted that very much. There was nothing in her family history to indicate that.

The way the baby was lying? It was still so small! Surely that would have no bearing on things!

It had to be something else. Something she hadn't thought of. Something scary, no doubt—because that was how her life had played out so far, and she knew that whatever it was she was going to be facing it alone, so...

The staff room was full of staff waiting for the hand-over. Nervously she let her gaze scan the room, but she didn't see Logan and she felt herself relax a little. No matter what had happened between them, she still needed to continue her education.

'Ellie! Hey, how are you feeling? Any better? You look a little pale.'

She smiled at the nurse. 'Just tired, that's all. It was a long night.'

'Well, I hope it's nothing catching.' The nurse smiled.

Was grief catching? Pregnancy certainly wasn't. But grief and hurt and pain might be. It often caught people unawares. Knocked them sideways—wasn't that what they said? Life throwing you a curveball? Having to roll with the punches?

Well, she was fed up with having to do that. What had she done in life that made her deserve all this?

She sat down and Dr Curtis from the night shift stood up at the front. He waited for them to settle and stop talking and then began the hand-over, going over each case, what treatment they'd had overnight, any issues and any red flags. He listed the tests that still needed doing, and the procedures certain babies were due for.

'And as you'll see we have no Dr Riley with us this morning. He's swapped to nights for the next couple of weeks, so we'll just have to cope without him.'

Everyone grumbled—but not Ellie. *Swapped to nights?* Because of what had happened with *them*? Who would be there overnight for Rachel? There must be someone. His parents? A friend? Who? Perhaps there was someone else? Some other relationship he was in and that was why he'd got so vehement with her the other day. Because he'd been juggling two women at the same time. It wouldn't be the first time a man had done that.

She raised a hand. 'He was my learning mentor. Who do I go to now if my shifts haven't been changed to match his?'

'Ah, yes, he mentioned that. You'll now be with me—but you haven't got long left on this placement, and Dr Riley has assured me your training has been proceeding well, so it shouldn't disturb you too much. Okay?'

No. No, it *wasn't* okay. But she nodded anyway. She guessed she'd probably never meant that much to him anyway.

Logan's mother, now back from her travels in Bali, had been really keen to catch up with her granddaughter and had offered to come over each evening and be around through the night, whilst he was at work. She'd been happy to have the company and not be alone at night, what with his dad now being away on a golfing trip to Sri Lanka. His mum hated being alone, so it was a solution that fitted them all.

'I promise it's just for the next couple of weeks or so. You should be home again for when Dad gets back from his trip.'

'Oh, it's no problem! I love being here for you and Rachel—you know that. But is everything all right? I thought they knew you couldn't do nights?'

'They do. It's just... I offered.'

'Oh. Are you sure everything is all right?'

He nodded, but he had to turn away. She could always tell when he was lying. But what was he going to do? Tell her he was trying to give Ellie Jones some space for a bit? The woman he'd got pregnant? That didn't sound very good, did it?

But he'd done it for Ellie. For her education. He'd screwed up what they had, but he wasn't going to mess with her career. That was important to her. So he'd swapped shifts for her benefit. This way she could continue with her placement without the distraction of him, and concentrate on what she had to do to pass without him ruining everything for her.

Why did he keep doing that to her? He'd left her to go to Edinburgh for his own education and now he was walking away again for the benefit of *hers*!

It was ridiculous! But he would do it because it was best for her. And, despite what he'd done, he did want the best for her. Of course he did. She needed someone who could be there for her one hundred percent, and he couldn't do that if he was distracted by his own feelings for her. She probably didn't understand right now, but she would.

Yes, he loved Ellie. He always had. He'd always cared for her. Deeply. He knew that. It had been hard to walk away from her the first time and he'd fought so hard not to contact her—because what would that have achieved? So he'd told himself he didn't love her because

that was better, wasn't it? Easier for his con-
science to bear?

And then there'd been Jo, and then Rachel,
and then Ellie again, and…

He'd never be able to adequately explain just
how he'd felt to have Ellie back in his life again.
That first day, seeing her standing there on
his ward in The Nest, looking so alone… He'd
wondered what that look in her eyes had been
about and he got it now. Seeing all those babies
after losing her own must have been terrifying.
How brave she was to go through this—and
now she was pregnant. With *his* child!

He would be there for them both. He would!

But the big question was, would she ever understand the sacrifice he was making?

He was so afraid. Afraid of allowing himself
to love her fully, freely, knowing that something could happen to her at any time and rip
his heart from his chest and bring him to his
knees. He'd been through it with Jo and barely
kept going, but he had done so because he'd
needed to be a father. To sit by the incubator holding his own daughter in The Nest. The
team had been by his side and had been wonderful, but at the end of the day it had all been
down to him.

What if something terrible happened to
Ellie or the baby? What if this baby had renal

agenesis, too? He wasn't brave enough to take a chance on experiencing another loss. How many losses could one person go through before they were unable to function?

These thoughts weighed heavy on his mind as he made his way to work, making sure he saw Ellie leave before he entered the building for his shift. His heart had missed a beat at the sight of her. She looked so forlorn. So lost. So weary. All this had to be weighing heavily on her and he wanted to be there, to wrap his arms around her and tell her that no matter what it would be all right.

But he was afraid to go to her. To make it worse. So he stood back.

His first patient to check on, Baby Wells, was a new admission. Just twenty-five weeks' gestation, tiny as a baby bird, and covered in the usual tubes, monitors and oversized hat. He saw that one of the team had given him a knitted octopus to hold on to. They found that a lot of babies found comfort in knitted toys. They mimicked the feel of the long umbilical cord they'd felt in the safety of the womb.

'Hello…' he said in a low voice to the mother who sat alongside. 'I'm Dr Logan Riley and I'll be looking after your little one tonight. Does he have a name yet?'

'No. But I've been considering a couple.'

'What are they?'

'I've always liked the name Conor, but I wonder if I ought to name him after his father.'

Logan nodded. He'd read in the notes that the father had passed away. In a way, this baby's mother was in the position he'd found himself in a long, long time ago. He wanted to be able to tell her that it would all work out, but he didn't know that. Not for sure. And it was always best never to make promises you couldn't keep.

'What was his dad's name?'

'Mitchell.'

'Both good names. Strong. Which do you think suits him best?'

She smiled, her eyes welling up. 'Mitchell.'

He offered her a box of tissues. 'Let me know when you've chosen and we can update his records.'

'Okay.' She wiped her nose and dabbed at the undersides of her eyes. 'You know he died just a few months ago? My husband?'

Logan nodded.

'He was so excited about this pregnancy. We both were. We'd already been through so much—three miscarriages. *Three!* I didn't want to try again. I even went on the pill. But then *he* came along.' She smiled down at her baby.

'Despite everything, I guess he was meant to be, huh?'

Ellie had been on the pill and got pregnant. He couldn't help but think of her.

'Were your miscarriages early on?'

She shook her head. 'No. Second trimester. I had to give birth to them all.'

Logan sank into his seat as he tried to imagine that. What she must have been through.

'But then Mitchell, here—well, he made it to twenty-five weeks and they rushed him up here. Do you have any idea just how much I want to be able to hold a baby of my own in my arms?'

He nodded. 'I think I can imagine.'

'Well, times that by a hundred. A thousand. To lose all those babies and then my husband, and then to go into early labour with this one... I was so scared!'

'But brave, too.' He smiled. How much courage must this woman have found to keep on enduring? Doing it alone? 'How do you think you managed it?'

She smiled. 'You just have to, you know? It's not a question of walking away. You love them and you try your best, no matter what.'

No matter what.

Was that the answer? You just kept going? Because there was no other option? He loved Rachel and he had to love Ellie and the baby, because this staying away, this walking away, had hurt him so badly he could hardly breathe.

Was he doing it for her? Or was he doing it to preserve himself?

I've been selfish!

Ellie needed him! His baby needed him! He should never have walked away! Especially knowing how she'd been abandoned before.

Logan gritted his teeth, wanting to go straight to his office and call her right now. But he couldn't. It was the middle of the night. He felt ashamed of his own selfish behaviour. How would he face her? Apologise? Explain?

'So, it's Mitchell, after all?'

The mother smiled and nodded. Clearly glad to have made the decision.

'I'll change his tags. Let's make it official.'

Ellie was nearly at the end of her first trimester now, and already her waistbands were getting tight. Perhaps it was just all this eating she was doing to stave off the sickness she was feeling? It had to be that, right?

So why aren't I putting on weight everywhere else?

What *was* it? She feared it was some extremely rare condition she didn't know about. Something she hadn't yet come across in her textbooks and research.

Seated in the waiting room of the department, she found herself anxiously fidgeting with the strap of her handbag. She was constantly checking her mobile phone, and twiddling with the hem of her shirt. She was so absorbed that she didn't notice someone come and stand before her until his feet came into view.

She looked up. 'Logan!'

What was he doing here? *Oh, of course. He's here for the baby. Not me. Remember?*

'I wasn't sure you'd come.'

'I said I would.'

Yes, he'd made that quite clear. He wasn't here for her. He was here because he felt a responsibility for putting this probably incredibly ill baby into her womb.

'But I'm also here to explain, if you'll let me.'

Was he really going to string this out even more? What was there left for them to say to one another? Did he not know how hard it was for her to have him here? The man she loved? The man she had in her heart but couldn't have in her arms?

'Oh?'

He sank down into the chair next to her. 'The last time we spoke I said something that I couldn't properly explain. I was speaking from a place of fear. I acted the way I did because

I was trying to protect you from what might come. From the knowledge that I had to be strong for you if everything went wrong.'

He shifted in his seat, made sure she was looking at him and took both her hands in his. She had to hear what he had to say.

'I lost the woman I loved when she was pregnant and I nearly lost my child, too. I've never been so scared in my entire life, Ellie. And when that happened I couldn't imagine going through the same thing again. Knowing how it would hurt you, I took a step back, thinking that if everything went wrong I'd be strong enough to support you—*if* I had some distance. I was bouncing from one thought and feeling to another, like a ball in a pinball machine, and in some stupid, confused, terrified act of trying to distance myself I did what I did and broke your heart. I never meant to. I'm sorry. And I'd like to hope you could learn to forgive me.'

She held her breath, listening to him speak. 'I...'

'I didn't realise until I'd done what I did that you would feel I was abandoning you again, so I've come to tell you that I'm not just here for the baby but for *you* too—whatever happens when we go into that room. I'm here for *us*. If you'll let there *be* an us. And to prove what I mean by that I'd like to do this...'

He got down on one knee and reached into his pocket.

She heard gasps of delight from the other mums-to-be in the room and felt her cheeks colour as he produced a small red velvet box and opened it to reveal a diamond solitaire.

'I love you, Ellie Jones. I always have and I always will. I want you in my life for ever. I want to show the whole world how committed we are. I want to spend the rest of my life showing you every day just how much I love you and how much you mean to me. Will you marry me?'

The room went silent, except for the ringing of a phone at the main desk, and Ellie watched as the receptionist picked up the handset as if in slow motion, her mouth agape, waiting for her answer.

He *loved* her? He'd been *scared*? Well, so had she! Terribly afraid!

But didn't they all do silly things when they were scared? She'd tried to close her whole life off because of what had happened with Samuel and Daniel. She'd been spending all her free hours glued to the internet, trying to discover all the obscure pregnancy-related complications there had ever been so that she could be prepared for each individual occurrence, should it happen.

That wasn't rational behaviour! That was ridiculous! She'd almost driven herself insane, searching for what might be wrong with this pregnancy, when she'd been given no hint that there was anything wrong at all just yet!

And best of all he'd said that he loved her. That he was here for her no matter what. They could both go into that ultrasound room and hear the worst news of their entire lives but he wanted to be by her side for it. He'd been trying to be strong for her by creating some space for himself. That was all. He'd done it all for *her*.

'What about Rachel?'

'I've spoken to Rachel. She knows I'm doing this and she's happy about it. She said, *"At least you won't be lonely any more."* But please don't say yes because you think you'll make Rachel happy, or me happy. Say yes only if you mean it. If you want me as much as I want you. If you *love* me as much as I love you.'

Her heart was pounding in her chest and slowly a smile emerged onto her face. 'Yes! Of course, *yes!*'

The room erupted into noise as he slid the ring onto her finger, and then he was leaning forward to kiss her and hug her.

Words were not enough to explain how she felt in that moment as she stood there, her arms wrapped around the man she loved. Her happiness had multiplied suddenly, exponentially, and if the room had had no lights she felt sure her smile would have lit the place up instead.

They settled into chairs next to each other and she fiddled with the solitaire on her finger. 'It's beautiful…' She kissed him, feeling her heart expand to let him in, feeling the warmth and the strength of his love surround her. Whatever faced them they would do it together.

'Ellie Jones?' said a voice.

A woman stood in the doorway of the ultrasound room. It was her turn.

She turned to face Logan. 'Are we ready for this?'

He squeezed her hand tight and placed another kiss on her lips. 'We can face anything. No matter what.'

Ellie lay down on the bed and undid the button and the zip on her jeans. To be quite frank it was a relief. She'd stuffed herself into them that morning, figuring they would do for the rest of the week, but she'd been regretting that decision ever since she'd left home.

Now she lay there, flinching as cold gel was squirted onto her lower abdomen and the sonographer placed the probe.

She didn't have to reach for Logan's hand. He already held her hand in his and now he kissed it reassuringly. She smiled at him, and then bit her lip. She couldn't see the screen, but she could see the sonographer frowning and her spirits sank.

She mentally prepared herself for the worst. 'What is it? You can tell me.'

The sonographer shook her head. 'I'm…er… this is my first day going solo and I think I just need someone to double-check something for me.'

Ellie *knew* it. She'd known there was something wrong!

'Do you have any history of multiples in your family?' asked the sonographer.

She blinked. Multiples? 'Er… I'm sorry? What…? Er…no.' She glanced at Logan, who shook his head.

'Nor me, as far as I know. Is it twins?'

Ellie turned back to the sonographer, who was shaking her head with a huge smile upon her face.

'I think it *is*!'

Twins!

A multiple pregnancy!

That had to explain why she was so much bigger! She had dismissed that idea simply because there wasn't any history of twins in her family, and quite frankly it had seemed too easy a solution. She'd automatically focused on the dark and the horrible, because that was all she'd ever experienced.

'Twins…?'

'I think so. I'll just get my colleague to confirm…to make sure I'm not missing anything.'

Ellie began to shake. 'Okay…'

The sonographer nipped out of the room and Ellie turned to face Logan. 'Oh, my God! *Twins!*'

He laughed. 'I know! That's *crazy*!'

The sonographer came back with a colleague, who sat down and moved the probe once again before turning the screen and showing them their babies, counting them off—one and two—as she scanned.

'Are they okay? I've been so worried about bilateral renal agenesis. My son had it and—'

'Everything looks okay so far. All good. They're each the size of a singleton baby at this gestation.'

'Oh, my God!' Tears of relief began to flow freely down her cheeks. They were okay! They were healthy! She had *two* babies inside her!

'This will probably explain why your abdomen is a little larger than we'd expect at this stage.'

'Are they identical?' asked Logan.

The sonographer moved the probe. 'See this? They're in individual sacs, so no.'

Logan shook his head in awe. In amazement. He leant forward and kissed Ellie, passing her a tissue for her tears. 'Are you happy?'

'Are you kidding me? I'm *ecstatic*. This day has gone so much better than I could ever have imagined.'

He smiled and kissed her forehead, stroking back her dark hair. 'I'm glad. It's been one of the best days of my life so far.'

'You mean it?'

He smiled. 'Of course I do.'

And then he kissed her again.

EPILOGUE

LOGAN KNELT DOWN to face Rachel outside the hospital room. 'Now, before we go in, tell me the rules again.'

'Be gentle.'

'And…?'

'Wash my hands.'

He smiled. 'Okay. If we press this button on the wall it'll help us do that.'

He demonstrated how to get some antibacterial hand gel from the wall dispenser and rubbed his hands, watching Rachel as she did the same.

'And what else do we need to be?'

Rachel smiled. 'Quiet. Can I see the babies now?'

'Sure.' He elbowed the door open, beaming a smile at Ellie, who sat between two incubators, a blanket over her lap. 'Hey!'

'Rachel!' Ellie beamed a smile and reached out with her hands, curling her little fingers.

She and Rachel had found a new way to give each other hugs that didn't make Rachel feel uncomfortable with bodily contact. They made pinkie promises. Hooking their pinkie fingers around each other's.

'How are you doing, pumpkin?'

'I'm not a pumpkin, Ellie. I'm a little girl.'

She laughed. 'Of course you are. Silly me. I forgot. I saw your beautiful smile and couldn't help myself.'

'Is this my sister and brother?' Rachel peered at each incubator, her expression curious and interested.

They were in The Nest, of course. Not because anything was wrong, but because the twins had been born at thirty-six weeks—early for a singleton pregnancy, but perfect for a twin one. It was purely for monitoring. To make sure they maintained their temperature and oxygen levels and until they learned the sucking reflex for their feeds.

'Yes. This one is Holly and the boy over here is... Well, we wondered if *you'd* like to be the one to give him a name?'

Ellie and Logan had discussed this. There were so many names they both liked, but they wanted Rachel to feel as if she had a part in this new family, and that meant including her in their decisions. Allowing her to name one of the babies was a huge thing, and something they hoped would allow her to feel closer to her new siblings.

Rachel took a good, hard look at him. 'He's very small.'

'He's very young.'

'He looks like a baby.'

They laughed. 'He *is* a baby!'

'Hmm…'

Logan looked at Ellie and smiled as his daughter thought of a good name for their son.

It had been non-stop since they'd found out they were having twins. There'd been extra medical checks and explaining everything to Rachel—including the fact that Ellie would be moving in to their home and that they'd be getting married.

Ellie didn't want to be a pregnant bride, so their wedding wasn't until next year, but the buying of two of everything, whilst they were both working, and Ellie's carrying two babies had been a whirlwind of appointments, scans, shifts at the hospital and scratching their heads over flat-pack furniture.

Ellie had brought Samuel's crib with her. They were going to give it to their son. Whatever he was going to be called.

Logan suddenly had a scary thought. 'Please

don't name him anything medical, Rachel. I don't want a son named Aorta, or anything.'

Rachel smiled. 'Don't be silly, Daddy. I know how to choose a boy's name.'

'Oh. Right. Okay.' He couldn't help but smile at her admonishment.

Her little face was screwed up in concentration, and then suddenly her brow unfurrowed and a huge smile came across her face. 'Okay. I know his name!'

'What is it?' Ellie asked, looking at Logan nervously.

'Tobias. Tobias Samuel.' Rachel looked at them both, very pleased with her choice.

Logan nodded and looked at Ellie to see if that was all right. They'd discussed giving their son Samuel's name as a middle name, but for Rachel to choose it… Well, that meant so much more.

'That's perfect, Rachel,' Ellie said, tears of happiness in her eyes. 'Holly and Tobias.'

'We have his present, Daddy—remember?' Rachel grabbed the gift bag from her father's hand and placed it on Ellie's lap. 'We brought him this. For his crib.'

Ellie frowned and opened the bag, and Logan watched as she gasped and tears welled up, reaching in to pull out the blue teddy bear that had sat in Samuel's room all alone for all this time.

Ellie hugged it to her and kissed it as her tears dripped onto the bear's head.

'Have I upset you?' Rachel asked.

'No. No, darling, you haven't. You've made me the happiest and proudest mummy in the whole world.'

And she got up, kissed the bear, and carefully placed it in Tobias's crib.

Where it had always been meant to be.

* * * * *

If you enjoyed this story, check out these other great reads from Louisa Heaton

Their Unexpected Babies
Saving the Single Dad Doc
A Child to Heal Them
Pregnant with His Royal Twins

All available now!